Uprising Book 1 – Earth Awakening

Book 1 in the Uprising series

For Izzy and Lou... as Rod said
The first cut is the deepest.☺

Copyright © 2023 Alan Glyn Smith
All rights reserved.

Contents

Uprising Book 1 – Earth Awakening 1
Chapter 1 7
Chapter 2 20
Chapter 3 29
Chapter 4 46
Chapter 5 65
Chapter 6 88
Chapter 7 139
Chapter 8 158
Chapter 9 193
Chapter 10 202
Chapter 11 253
Chapter 12 275
Chapter 13 287
Epilogue 314

Chapter 1

Wing Commander (retd) Paul Arwyn, 35 stood outside his "work in progress" of a Breton farmhouse.

Leaning heavily on his walking stick he stooped and looked a lot shorter than his normal six foot two inches. He was dark haired, brown eyed, intelligent, well read and with a good sense of humour. He used to keep fit, until the accident, but he had gone to seed recently he'd lost weight and looked gaunt and grey.

Izzy, his loyal companion, a German shepherd of around 2 years old, sat by his feet.

Izzy, he looked down at her and managed a weak smile. What a wonderful friend and companion a beloved member of his family, his pack?

He smiled inwardly remembering the moment he and Izzy had met...

It was a cold wintry night and he'd been out shopping late to the local hypermarket. It was dark and rain blew in from the Bay of Biscay. Driving back to the house he spotted a bundle at the side of the road that hadn't been there before. "Bloody fly tippers" he thought. But as he passed he thought he saw it move. Coming to a halt he reversed back, sat and watched.

Yes it had moved!

He slowly got out of his Land Rover. He only had two speeds these days, slow and stop. A bit of a come down from his days as Royal Air Force Wing Commander Arwyn, in charge of the famous 617 squadron of F35 Lightning II's flying around at 1200 mph. His father had flown the original English Electric Lightning of 11 squadron and he was now the second generation of Lightning pilots.

Pulling his collar up to shelter from the rain, he walked or rather limped across to the bundle and pulled back the smelly cloth, to his shock looking back at him were the two beautiful brown eyes of a young German shepherd It couldn't have been more than a couple of months old.

It was soaking wet, shivering and whining so quietly he could barely hear it. It feebly tried to lick his hand with a look of sadness that took his breath away and broke his heart, it was crying out for help, he managed to remove the cloth, and other bits of rubbish, and slowly, trying to ignore the pain in his back and leg, he picked the dog up.

Whimpering slightly, Paul that is, not the dog, he managed to get it over to the Land Rover. He got the back door open and put *her* in (yes he'd checked...) got back into the cab and set off back home.

"Louise, Louise, come here quickly I need some help" he shouted.

"What is it" she asked a moment later, coming out of the house while pulling her fleece on.

"Have a look..." He said pointing to the back door.

She stepped towards the car, opened the door and putting her hand up to cover her mouth said "Oh my..." her expression filling with compassion and love.

"Let's get her into the house"

Together they carried her into the kitchen. Louise ran upstairs to get some quilts and blankets and laid them down in front of the log burner. The dog was so malnourished you could see almost every bone in her body.

Paul got some cold chicken left over from the previous night's dinner out of the fridge and poured a bowl of water.

The poor thing couldn't stand so he held small pieces to her mouth which she licked, then, realising what it was, she ate some. Several mouthfuls later she raised her head to drink some water from the bowl. Paul had to admire her spirit.

"Who would do such a thing as to starve and abandon a beautiful dog like her?" he asked.

"No Idea, but they don't deserve to live" Louise replied.

He settled into the comfy chair next to the fire and watched her for a while. Fatigue washed over him, he hadn't realised how late it was and how tiring a day it had been.

"What should we do with her?" Lou asked.

"I think we should keep her." Paul said.

"Fine by me" she smiled.

He watched her for a while and fell into a deep sleep.

He woke to a strange sensation, he looked down and there was the dog standing on four shaky legs licking his hand. He smiled at her.

Morning sunlight was streaming through the windows into the kitchen. The fire had gone out a while ago but he stood up slowly and stretched the kinks out of his back, swallowed a couple of his Tramadol tablets and fetched the dog some more of the chicken for her breakfast which she managed to stand up for.
He watched her as she wolfed it down...

"Don't get used to it, it's not going to be Chicken every day" he laughed as he gingerly hobbled around, kneeling down to get a fire going before fixing up coffee and toast.

"Well that was a memorable night. If she's staying what shall we call her. Got any ideas?" He asked Lou over breakfast.

"Izzy, we should call her Izzy." Lou said it so quickly Paul was a little taken aback.

"Wow, why so certain?" Paul asked.

"Izzy was a dog I had as a child who I loved to bits. We were inseparable and it broke my heart when she passed on, it seems so unfair. They are here with us, share everything with us, give us unconditional love and are taken away from us all too soon."

"Fair enough, Izzy it is." he said.

"Hey Izzy," Paul said, leaning over and stroking her head. She looked up at him, gave him another lick and laid down on what was now, not theirs, but *her* blankets, took a huge breath and blew it out in the way only a German Shepherd can exhale relaxation and acceptance... she'd found her forever home.

Breaking out of his reverie, Paul took a couple of deep breaths and released them slowly trying to ease the pain in his lower back or at least try and tune it out. Allowing it to wash through him he managed to get a moment of respite and set off towards the house. Izzy followed closely as usual.

It was a fixer upper no doubt about that. He'd bought it with money he had saved along with a pension from the RAF and compensation from the car crash. He wasn't a millionaire but he was ok.

He lived there with Louise who was a professional artist, tall, mid thirties, with long dark brown hair, dark brown eyes, a wonderful smile that lit up the room oh, and a fabulous figure.

What she had seen in him he could never understand. But he'd fallen for her immediately.

They moved in about two years ago intending to settle down, possibly even start a family who knew? It was exciting and wonderful to start with... But fate wasn't having any of that nonsense... no sir.

His car accident that caused his early retirement from the RAF had occurred exactly two years, seven months and six days ago (not that he was counting ha! No bitterness at all...) he hadn't been at fault, a lorry driver who had been driving for too long and fell asleep at the wheel crashed into the side of his car, pinning him for over an hour in agonising pain before the fire brigade could extract him.

Five weeks in hospital, emergency surgery on his spine and left leg had left him with damaged vertebrae pins and plates in his femur and in constant pain ever since. On the bad days he needed a walking stick to get around on the better ones, which seemed to be fewer and further between, it was easier.

The first few months he was ok he managed the pain and almost led a normal life. It was nice, together they organised the refurbishment of the old Breton farmhouse. The electrical system, the plumbing, a new bathroom and kitchen which they chose together which gave Paul a feeling of togetherness of being part of a team again "I could get used to this" he thought and smiled to himself. However, dark clouds were gathering and Paul was still taking his pain meds...

Days passed into weeks, addiction and its associated symptoms began to appear. Louise was nagging him about taking the tablets, he was fine and he could manage it, if only she wouldn't nag so!

And so it began, the steady decline, the increasing arguments, the certainty that Louise was doing something behind his back, that she would take away his meds or worse report him to someone. He couldn't see how irrational he had become.

Six months later, the increasing paranoia, his erratic mood swings and his general decline had prompted her to issue an ultimatum. It was her or the drugs... Louise had finally had enough. She gave him another week and at the end of that time he hadn't attempted to get help or ditch the drugs. So with huge regrets and great reluctance, she packed her clothes and other essentials, left instructions with a removal company to collect some items of furniture of hers and moved back to the UK.

That was a week ago. He opened the front door and stepped inside. Suddenly the pain of the separation, of his injuries, of his life being cut short, of his future being taken away from him hit him hard, he staggered into the house, tears flowing down his cheeks. How could he carry on like this?

Stumbling across the kitchen he grabbed the packets of tablets from the shelf not really knowing what he wanted to do other than stop it all, end the pain both physical and mental. He staggered over to the fire, Izzy shadowing him and looking up into his eyes not knowing how to comfort or help her man. He sat in the comfy chair and saw that Izzy was looking at him intently.

"What's up sweetie?" he asked barely able to focus on her lovely face as tears filled his eyes.

She whined at him and raised a paw and touched his hand where he clutched the painkillers.

He looked at it, realisation hitting home. He got angry. Shit! What was he doing? How had it come to this?

He leaned over, opened the log burner door and threw the tablets on the fire.

He held his head in his hands and cried like a baby letting out all the pent up anger, self pity and heartache he had experienced over the last couple of years.

The only comfort he had was Izzy and she didn't disappoint. She nuzzled his face and whined as he sat up and through the tears he laughed spraying snot everywhere which made him laugh even more. He stood up, cleaned himself with some kitchen towel, went upstairs, got into bed and fell asleep.

Morning arrived with an Atlantic storm blowing in. the wind and rain howling against the house, shaking the trees and rattling the windows.

His body ached all over. All he could think of was getting some of his tablets. He turned over painfully, slowly, reaching into the bedside drawer.

Then he remembered last night. Dammit he'd burned all of them. Why did he do something so stupid? He could have simply cut down on them gradually over the next week or two?

A voice at the back of his mind said "Really? Oh yeah right that would have happened... NOT"

He realised, whatever that voice was, it was right. No it wouldn't have happened he had to get this monkey off his back once and for all. Perhaps if he was clean he and Lou might get back together?

Not really knowing what to do next he got up and used the bathroom managing to clean his teeth, which made him feel a little better.

He went downstairs, Izzy following closely as usual not taking her eyes off him for a second. As if she knew something bad was happening and didn't know what to do other than be there with him.

He noticed her and for the first time his RAF officer training kicked in. It had instilled a sense of duty and responsibility towards your team and Izzy certainly was part of the team.

 "An army marches on its stomach hey kid?" He smiled a thin smile at Izzy and grabbed a tin of dog food.

Izzy fed, he brewed a coffee and sat in a kitchen chair staring out of the window at the raging storm. What was he going to do next?

He decided to Google what happens when coming off an opioid painkiller.

He wished he hadn't ... anxiety, insomnia, drug cravings, body aches, sweating, yawning, runny nose, teary eyes, chills, goosebumps, stomach cramps, nausea, and diarrhoea. Oh good so much to look forward to!

The storm outside was blowing harder so he tried to occupy himself by reading or watching YouTube or TV.

It was dark by now and he'd been cooped up inside all day. He made coffee and drank it at the kitchen table.

He stood to go and wash the cup, turning around; he fell over Izzy who as always was following him closely.

He hit the floor hard the pain was excruciating and his brain decided enough was enough, it was having a time out and he slipped into unconsciousness.

He came to a while later. Not knowing how long he'd been out. Slowly he turned, everything hurt, his back, his leg. He was sure even his hair hurt! He lay back down, Izzy by his side, not moving an inch she hadn't left him the whole time. He reached over and touched her head scratching under her chin just as she liked.

"Thanks kid" he managed to say and smiled a little.

He remembered there were some paracetamol tablets in the kitchen drawer.

"Well perhaps not got the kick of an opium painkiller but beggars can't be choosers" he muttered.

He turned over slowly and got onto his knees. Using the table as a prop he stood up and worked his way to the dresser drawer. Fumbling around he found and downed a couple of tablets.

"Let's see if they have any effect, ey Izz?" Izzy looked at him and woofed, a low quiet noise as if to signify "yeah right!" It made him chuckle.

The storm had abated and after twenty minutes of sitting in the comfy chair he decided to take Izzy for her usual walk.

"Come on kid, let's see if this takes my mind off things a bit" Izzy sprang up and tail wagging went straight to the back door sniffing and giddy with excitement. Nothing she liked better than going for a walk with her man.

Grabbing a torch and a waterproof coat he managed to struggle into his wellingtons using his walking tick, he hobbled out of the house. Closing the door behind him he turned slowly and trudged down the garden and out towards the woods, Izzy shooting ahead sniffing out all the good smells, the rabbits, the occasional fox or a deer all new, adding her own contribution on more than one occasion!

The wood next to the house contained an ancient burial site or Dolmen. They were scattered all across the ancient Celtic lands. Brittany, Cornwall, Wales, Ireland, Scotland.

It was reputed to be at least 4-5000 years old and although it sounded interesting and scary at the same time it was just four or five rocks arranged in a pile. Once you'd seen one you'd seen them all.

The site was a protected area however; the quarry behind the woods didn't seem to take any notice of that. Way to go big business thought Paul… It seemed to be creeping slowly towards the boundary getting closer all the time and Paul reckoned it may start affecting the dolmen and the woods in the next year or so.

Coming around a bend in the path he noticed it didn't look the same as usual. Stretching from the side near the woods to the other was a dark pile of something. He approached cautiously, the storm had uprooted a couple of trees next to the dolmen and a mini landslide had covered the path extending as far as the edge of the quarry.

"Oh well that's as far as we should go tonight Izzy" he called and Izzy turned back towards him.

He turned to go back to the house when a glint of light from the torch caught something on the floor amongst the tree roots.

Moving closer he saw a spherical object caked in mud. It shone in the torchlight. No bigger than his hand, he bent gingerly and picked it up an odd warm feeling came over him. It felt like he was being observed? Tested? He turned around a full three hundred and sixty degrees shining the torch into the distance but he couldn't see anything or anyone.

"Weird" he said aloud. He put the artefact in his pocket and turned to walk back home
Already feeling a tad better, the pain had eased a little so he put the kettle on, fed Izzy, and decided he'd eat something more substantial so he made himself a cheese sandwich.

He sat in the comfy chair to eat his meal, sharing most of the cheese with Izzy of course. Then he remembered the artefact. Standing up slowly, because he usually paid the price for sudden movement with a fair amount of pain, he removed it from his coat pocket and brought it back to the table.

It was a solid sphere caked in mud. He ran some water in a bowl, and set to with a cloth and scrubbing brush. Five minutes later he was astounded by what he saw.

The sphere was beautiful. It was smooth almost to the point of being frictionless which was very strange.

There were carvings? Or were they etchings? He didn't know how you would describe them inlaid into the surface. They had no edge as if they were fused into the sphere as part of the whole.

There was the image of a... a human? He wasn't sure. It looked more like an elf from one of those fantasy movies and two white dogs with red ears? It was beautiful but odd. What was it made of glass, resin? He hadn't a clue. Still, it was remarkably pretty and he got a stronger sense of a presence and of warmth and comfort when he held it.

"Oh well come on kid let's call it a day" he said to Izzy.

He put the orb on the dresser and took himself off to bed.

Chapter 2

This night, things were happening out in space. They should have happened a long, long time ago.

A large decelerating object approached Earth. Its trajectory would take it into a geostationary orbit about a thousand kilometres above the surface of the planet.

It was approximately four kilometres long by two kilometres wide by one kilometre deep. It was a silver grey colour and had numerous, what looked like antennae, and multiple bumps, dings, scrapes and dimples along its scarred and scoured surface.
It looked old. A long hump that ran the length of the ship from back to front ended in an orifice. Offset to one side sat another more obvious looking weapon any earth person would have immediately guessed cannon?

It was in fact very old, nearly ten thousand years old.

It was a ship belonging to an ancient race called, The Madden or at least that's what, in their language, to English ears it sounded like.

Silently and smoothly it continued to decelerate, finally coming to a halt.

It was massive, by now all of earth's major powers would be scrambling every fighter, alerting every missile battery and nuclear submarine and recalling all personnel back to base.

But Earth continued its daily routine, no one was any the wiser. Radar was harmlessly absorbed by its outer hull. Even visual telescopes couldn't see it as light was carefully refracted around the ship rendering it effectively invisible to the naked eye. There wasn't even a heat signature; it was at the same temperature as the surrounding space.
In essence no one knew of its presence...

Except...

Izzy stirred uneasily in her sleep, yelping quietly and paws twitching as if chasing something. Paul also moaned and moved around sweat beading on his brow. His movements became more powerful until moving a little too quickly he caused pain to erupt in his lower back.

Cursing loudly he was awake...

"What a weird dream that was" Izzy looked at him

"You too hey?" And he laughed ruffling her head.

He looked at the clock 4:30a.m. Get up or lay here? Get up. Lying in didn't help the back pain at all. In fact he felt pretty crap, any benefit he'd got from the paracetamol had long worn off.

Dragging himself downstairs he made a coffee and fed Izzy. Taking a couple of paracetamol he sat down at the kitchen table.

"Now what do I do?" He thought. He took a sip of coffee and exhaled trying to do some breathing meditation to relax his muscles and ease the pain.

A feeling of being watched hit him again as it did by the landslide last night and out of the corner of his eye he saw Izzy prick up her ears and tilt her head as if listening to something.

He turned around slowly, this time, getting goosebumps as if there was something behind him.

"Ah bugger," he said

"It's the withdrawal symptoms isn't it?"

"Damn I'm not going to enjoy this."

Assuming he was right he turned back to his coffee but he couldn't stomach it anymore.
He resumed the breathing technique and tried to relax. But the little prickle at the back of his mind wouldn't go away.

"Grrrr I'm getting really pissed off now" he shouted. He stood up, turned, picked up the coffee cup and hurled it at the dresser. The action caused him to twitch in pain as the cup shattered into smithereens in a satisfying way, but the uneasy feeling only grew stronger.

"This isn't *right*; the symptoms didn't include anything like this?"

Izzy whined and Paul looked at her. But she wasn't looking at him. Her focus was on the dresser. She was also doing that head tilt thingy when dogs look like they're asking a question?

"Curiouser and curiouser" he muttered.

Turning to look where Izzy was looking, the dresser, he couldn't work out what it was.

Something was different…

Then he saw it, a dull reddish glow coming from behind the large bowl that was stacked high with paperwork, bills, correspondence, small knickknacks and bits and pieces that had accumulated over time, the same pile that he'd always meant to but never actually sorted out.

Slowly he walked across the kitchen Izzy at his side, both of them totally focused on the glow. The sensation of being watched growing stronger and stronger the closer he got.

Moving aside the bowl there sat the orb glowing more brightly the closer he got. Or did he mean they got? Because he had no doubt that this orb was reacting to both him and Izzy and Izzy was certainly entranced by it.

He reached for it very slowly, afraid to touch it and at the same time he couldn't help but want to touch it.

"What the f…" he said "what is going on here?"

Izzy whined and licked her nose nervously.

Turning to her he said "What? You think I should pick it up?"

Izzy woofed gently once.

"Ok here goes…"

He reached out again and closed his hand around the orb.

A big fat nothing happened.

"Wow that was an anticlimax" he said to Izzy holding the orb in his hand. He turned and sat down at the table.

"Now what?"

The orb began to heat up he put it down before it burnt him but it didn't seem to get any hotter.

A dazzling light erupted in front of him and a holographic video stuttered into life. There was audio as well but it it sounded as if the recording was done with a malfunctioning microphone. He chuckled to himself remembering a British comedian who made his name doing the very same thing. *"Strange how one's brain works when you're under stress"* he thought

The holographic images continued to change but didn't really make sense until he saw a view he recognised immediately.

"Bloody hell, that's Snowdonia, the Rivals and the Menai Straits. What's going on here?"

The video stopped abruptly.

"Ah no!" He panicked thinking he'd broken it somehow.

He picked up the orb and noticed a small, oval area, brighter than the rest. Thinking it might be a control of some kind he touched it with his finger. Sure enough the same video ran again.

It showed the view of North Wales as if viewed from Anglesey and the same broken soundtrack.

He was filled with the overriding urge to go back to his homeland. He'd been born not far from Caernarfon in Gwynedd and he knew the area like the back of his hand.

Without knowing why he was doing this he turned and nearly ran upstairs to start packing.

"What the Fuck!" He stopped halfway up the stairs

"I'm not in pain?" he exclaimed in surprise.

The shock caused him to stagger, nearly losing his balance. He caught himself and stood leaning against the wall. What the hell was going on?

He walked slowly up the stairs. As he got near the bedroom he felt the pain return.

Going further on it began to get worse until it was back to its usual intensity.

He experimented and walked back towards the stairs. The pain diminished. He continued back down until he was back at the table again at which point the pain had gone...

"What the heck? What have I found?"

He sat down again. Not knowing what to do he picked up the orb and went back upstairs. Sure enough this time he remained pain free.

"Oh my god, this is incredible Izzy." He said

Joy and exhilaration exploded out of him, laughing out loud for the first time in a long time he bent down and cuddled Izzy, she responded, picking up the happiness in Paul's face and body language and she bounced around him as he whooped and hollered around the bedroom jumping up and down punching the air.

A minute later "fighter pilot Paul" had taken control and he calmed down.

"Let's think about this logically," he said.

"Obviously I should go to the authorities with this" But that just didn't feel right. He felt he had a big connection with the artefact especially as it had shown him his old home.

There was something odd about the video he couldn't quite put his finger on. What was it?

He pressed the, what he now called the 'play button'

He studied the video again and still he couldn't work out what was eluding him. As an RAF pilot he'd trained on fast jets at RAF Valley on Anglesey, he had flown over this area dozens of times at a similar height to what the video was showing.

Then he saw it... or rather he didn't... "There are no buildings!" he exclaimed.

Or more accurately there was no evidence of human beings at all, or at least where he expected them.

No Caernarfon, no Felinheli, no world famous Thomas Telford suspension bridge in fact the only signs of human habitation was when the camera panned down to reveal a henge and some standing stones directly below.

"What on earth is going on?"

"Surely the only way you could do this, would be to edit the buildings and roads and bridges and boats out of it?"

"But why would anyone bother?"

Then it struck him, how *could* anyone have done it? Created a very high quality aerial shot of North Wales then bury the device underground where it would only be revealed after a storm and a tree falling over? In fact, how long had that tree been there?

What about the dolmen? There had to be a link there somehow.

The image of the henge and the standing stones was the clue.

"Damn... this orb must be old."

He dug out his laptop. His brain was fizzing. He knew of a couple of places on Anglesey that could be the henge in question but neither quite fit.

One, Bryn Celli Ddu was the likeliest option but the video didn't show a burial mound and that was what he knew was at Bryn Celli Ddu.

Googling the site he began to read.

The site began over 5000 years ago as a henge. A ritual enclosure surrounded by a raised bank with a ditch on the inside enclosing a set of standing stones. That's exactly what the video was showing. The tomb wasn't built until later.

"Well bugger me!" He said, running his hands through his hair.

"Guess we're going on a road trip Izz" she barked and turned around as giddy as if she was going for a walk.

Chapter 3

Carrying the orb everywhere with him Paul packed a hold-all. Not knowing how long he would be away for.

He suddenly realised Izzy needed to visit the vet for her anti worming tablets before she could be admitted into the UK.

It was only 08:00 so he called the local vet who had looked after Izzy since she'd first arrived. No problem, they could fit her in this morning. That meant they couldn't cross until the following day at the earliest. Paul groaned in frustration he was champing at the bit and the delay was extremely annoying.

He opened his laptop and got out his debit card. He booked them both onto Eurotunnel midday tomorrow.

He couldn't wait. He was buzzing with excitement. What would he find when he got there? He didn't know what to expect.

"Oh well, we'll see what happens". He thought aloud.

He couldn't believe his good luck, the pain that had ruined his life for two years, but seemed like forever, had vanished.

He'd be ok as long as he kept the orb close. He'd tested it a couple of times and each time the pain returned if he moved more than 3-4 metres away.

At that moment a dark thought intruded. What if he was replacing a chemical crutch/death sentence for another, different, high tech version? He knew nothing about the orb. How was the orb nulling the pain? Would he become just as addicted to it? Would it eventually kill him as surely as the opiates would, and would it be an even more horrific death?

He shivered and shook himself. "No, not thinking about that. Not going there are we kid" he said looking at Izzy. She gave him a look he had not seen before it was a mixture of love and absolute certainty.

"What the heck! Now I'm imagining things about the dog, geez what next?"

Making sure the orb was in his pocket He drove to the vet and on the way called in on Elouan Mor, a mechanical genius. Elouan had rigged up the hydraulic/spring loaded contraption that allowed Izzy to easily get in and out of the back of his battered Land Rover at the touch of a button.

Elouan had a new winch to install.

"Bonjour Mr. Aroooin!" Elouan said, smiling at him as he came out of his workshop.

Paul smiled, for a Breton speaker, with the ties they had to Welsh, Cornish and other Celtic languages he couldn't get his tongue around Paul's Welsh surname Arwyn. Elouan Mor was a Breton by descent his surname meant "Sea" the same in Breton and Welsh

"Bonjour Elouan, ça va?"

"Oui très bien merci. You av ze Rover for ze winch yes? "

"Yes please, how long do you think to fit it?"

"I sink one hour? Maybe?"

" That would be perfect. Can I leave it here and come back later?"

"Oui pas de problème" he said

Elouan was a master mechanical engineer. He kept the Land Rover in fantastic condition with both engine and running gear purring smoothly. Paul had had the Land Rover altered to include a simple pull down camp-bed and cooker in the rear. With the addition of a chemical toilet and a plug in cooler it was a self contained, portable base of operations handy for long trips away, like now.

"Right, vet then supplies. Come on Izz" Said Paul opening the rear door and pressing the button to release the steps so Izzy could get down without jarring every joint in her body. He'd become quite attuned to physical impacts on body joints over the last couple of years and if he could make things easier for everyone he would.

Walking through his local town towards the vet, Izzy pulling on her lead he felt good for the first time in a long time. Even Izzy pulling hard didn't hurt his back.

But, it wasn't long before his darker, more pessimistic side stuck its oar in and said enjoy it while it lasts. It's too good to be true. You get nothing for free.

"Ah shut up" he said out loud earning a look from a passing local

"Sorry, not you!" He said, smiling apologetically and moved briskly on.

The vet took ten minutes, Izzy's passport all signed and stamped as required.

Supermarket next

He only wanted the essentials dog food, human food, candles, batteries, water, chocolate and a couple of beers.

An hour later he was back at Elouan's place. He was just finishing up.

He handed Paul a small remote control. It was a good winch with a capacity of 4500 kgs it could cope with most situations and was simple to operate, just how he liked things. A little easier than an F35 and a lot less training involved.

He shook Elouan's hand, loaded the supplies in the boxes under the drop down bed and got Izzy installed in her bed type platform behind and slightly below the tops of the front seats, a modification Izzy loved. She was safe, but could see everything, even when lying down.

"Thanks Elouan and see you soon" he called as he jumped into the driver's seat.

"Bon chance et bon courage Mr. Aroooin" Elouan replied, making Paul smile as they drove back home.

Morning couldn't come fast enough. He packed clothing and other essential gear, showered and went to bed.

He slept, but not brilliantly. A five o'clock alarm sounded and he rolled over to turn it off.

"Come on then kid let's get going." He said to the dog.

Two steps down the stairs a twinge of pain in his lower back made Paul remember the orb. "Damn. This is all going to take some getting used to" He muttered

Descending the stairs once more after retrieving the orb he let Izzy out into the garden to do her "business", made coffee, put Izzy's breakfast out and ate a croissant.

Shortly afterwards he turned off the water and electricity, closed and locked all the house shutters. Locked the front door and sat in the Land Rover just staring for a moment, taking time to let all of what had happened in just two days sink in.

Coming back to the present, "Onwards and upwards" he said. And turned the key, the Land Rover started beautifully, Elouan really was good, he thought.

Putting it in gear they set off for Calais.

The drive to Calais was uneventful apart from fuel and watering stops.

They arrived at the Eurotunnel check in. Did all the regular pet stuff, customs and passport control and before long they hit the motorway bound for North Wales.

Six hours later driving along the A55 towards Snowdonia Paul felt quite emotional coming home after so long. They crossed the Britannia Bridge over the Menai Straits. Turning left he drove into Llanfairpwllgwyngyllgogerwchwyndrobwllllantysiliogogogoch, or just Llanfair to the locals and on to Brynsiencyn where there used to be a pub called Y Groeslon if he remembered correctly?

Hopefully they could provide some accommodation. Otherwise it was kip in the car which, while reasonably comfortable with the alterations he'd had done, spending nights or even just one night in a cold vehicle was less preferable to a night indoors in a comfy bed.

The quiet country roads of Anglesey reminded him of home back in Brittany especially after the busy M25 and the rest of the UK's motorway network.

The hotel looked nice and inviting from outside. He grabbed his bag and Izzy's lead and let her out for a stretch.

"Better put your lead on girl. Don't want complaints before we're even booked in" he said rolling his eyes at how peculiar some people could be around dogs.

They entered the pub and immediately it went quiet. Paul glanced around the room at the people staring at him

"Mae hi'n oer heno ma" ("Its cold tonight") he said in Welsh, with a convincing local accent and smiled. The atmosphere changed immediately as everyone turned back to their meals, drinks and conversations. All except one man. He stared at Paul and wouldn't look away. He had a slightly disheveled appearance. Skinny with blonde hair and freckles, somewhere in his mid thirties he wore jeans and a red and black plaid shirt with decent walking boots completing the outdoorsy look.

He spoke to a middle aged lady who turned out to be the landlady. "Of course" she said, there was no problem with Izzy and a room was available out back.

After showing him to the room she returned to her other duties and left them in peace. Paul was bushed. Izzy wasn't much better. A quick walk for her and they'll turn in.

He put Izzy on her lead, grabbed some poo bags and left via the pubs rear door. It was cold and clear but moonless. They made their way slowly through the village.

Enjoying the walk and the fresh air Paul hadn't noticed that another person was behind them until he turned to go back to the pub.

The man was only five metres away and was coming straight towards Paul and Izzy. Before Paul had a chance to say anything the man spoke.

"What are you doing here, who are you. You shouldn't be here." Lifting a closed fist, he almost shouted these words without pausing for breath

Paul mentally reeled at the onslaught.

"Grrrrrrrr" the man stopped in his tracks and looked down his eyes wide when he saw Izzy whose head was down and her teeth were bared. It was the type of growl our ancient ancestors' dreaded hearing, connecting directly to the subconscious in a primal way that made hair stand up and bladders weaken.

Paul looked down at Izzy and said "Wow kid, didn't think you had that in you?" and chuckled

It seemed to break the ice because the stranger kind of deflated. His shoulders dropped and he uttered a huge sigh.

He recognised the man from the pub that wouldn't stop staring at him when he'd arrived. He had mentally labeled him "lumberjack man" due to the shirt and for a very brief second a famous comedy song jumped into his mind... shaking his head to rid himself of the thought he said

"Who do you think *you* are? Sneaking up on people like that in the street at night?" Paul asked

"Yes, sorry" he said "but there's something about you that is odd?"

"Like what?"

"You'll laugh if I tell you"

"Honestly" Paul chuckled "given the few days I've had, even if you told me little green men had kidnapped you and probed you, it wouldn't raise a titter"

The other man gawped at him. "Why... why would you say that?"

Paul paused and said "Why? Have you been kidnapped by little green men?"

"No... Not exactly." He said

Paul was suddenly intrigued and the same strange feeling he got when he first encountered the orb began prickling the back of his mind. He felt the feeling was important and he shouldn't ignore it. This sixth sense said *"trust him"*

"Look I'm staying at the pub let me buy you a pint and we can have a chat if that's ok with you?"

The stranger paused, considering Paul's offer. Then with a resigned shrug he said "Ok thanks why not."

They returned to the pub without sharing another word.

Ordering two pints of a nice local brew they found a secluded part of the bar. Izzy sat at Paul's feet between Paul and the stranger. It was obvious the stranger had had a few already but Paul didn't say anything.

"I'm Paul, and this is Izzy" he said, by way of introduction. "What's your story?"

"I'm Arawn, Arawn Griffiths." the man said.

Paul remembered the name from the Mabinogion he had read at school, Welsh folk stories; Arawn had been the Celtic god of war, revenge and the hunt. He was the ruler of Annwn, the hidden kingdom. Arawn hadn't been a particularly nice person. Paul remembered mention of people being hunted and other unpleasantness. He also remembered something about white dogs?

"Not as in the King of Annwn?" He said

"What do you know about Annwn?" Arawn asked, amazed that Paul knew the name.

"Only what I learned at school. I was born over on the mainland and went to school in Caernarfon?" He replied.

"Ah good, that's good" said Arawn nodding approvingly and taking a good drink.

"No one believes me they all laugh and scoff…" he continued, pausing for dramatic effect.

"Because… I… am the guardian of an ancient a secret"

Paul nearly choked on his drink and managed to turn it into a cough before Arawn took umbrage or got upset and left. He wanted to know more so he bit his lip and kept quiet.

"Many many generations ago over 240 actually, Aliens visited Earth…!"

He said it in a quiet voice so as not to be overheard but still managed to make it sound like a real "TADA" moment, the big reveal… he looked a little deflated and a tad miffed when Paul didn't react.

Angrily he said "I suppose that happens to you all the time?"

"Well, funny you should say that…" Paul muttered into his glass as he took another sip of beer.

"What does that mean?" Arawn asked.

"It's been a very strange few days and I get a feeling that what I'm about to say probably won't be a surprise to someone like you?"

"Huh, none taken..." Arawn replied

"Sorry, that came out wrong... What do you know about Bryn Celli Ddu?

Arawn went quiet and stared at Paul in a curious way as if he was sizing him up, judging him. He finally appeared to reach a conclusion and said

"Can you keep a secret?" Arawn asked.

"Well I have signed the Official Secrets Act, so yes I think so.?"

Arawn looked up at Paul again, then, glancing round the pub he whispered conspiratorially. "Can we meet here, outside in the car park, tomorrow? I would like to take you to see something. It's related to Bryn Celli Ddu"

Paul was very interested. "What time?"

"About ten o'clock?"

Not wanting to push, he saw and sensed Arawn's hesitation. So Paul agreed "That's fine, yes. In fact it's been a heck of a long day so I'm going to turn in"

"Ok, sleep well, see you tomorrow" Arawn said then downing the rest of his drink he got up and left.

Paul retired to his room. While getting ready for bed his mind wandered over the last few days. As unbelievable as it all seemed he didn't feel at all worried by any of it. It was almost as if it was natural, meant to be. He couldn't explain, but hopefully tomorrow might throw more light on it.

Crawling into the large double bed he fought with Izzy for some space. "Maybe we might make some sense of this hey kid" he said to Izzy, who opened one eye, took a huge breath and let it go as if to say "whatever" and settled down. Within seconds they were out for the count.

His phone alarm woke him at 7:30. Breakfast was served at 8:30 so time to walk Izzy. It was a nice day and Izzy loved the new smells the Welsh countryside had to offer. Clearing up after her, they returned to the pub and Paul had time for a shower and a shave.

He felt great; they went through to the bar where breakfast was a full fry up. Bacon, some excellent local sausage, mushrooms, eggs, fried bread and beans, a pot of tea, toast butter and marmalade… ha! He hadn't enjoyed his food so much in ages. Izzy loved it especially the sausages and looked so disappointed when Paul looked at her, laughed and said that was it "finis!"

By 10 o'clock Paul and Izzy were stood outside the pub raring to go.

Arawn arrived on time. "Morning" he said

"Bore da" said Paul. Izzy gave a short yip.

Arawn smiled "Good morning to you too Izzy"

"So," Paul asked "what do you want to show me?"

"It's not here; can we use your car? I don't have transport at the moment."

"Yes, no problem. Hop in" Paul said. Fishing his keys out of his pocket and blipping the Land Rover.

With Izzy in her usual position behind the front seats and Arawn giving the directions they moved off.

Less than ten minutes later, down a narrow country lane, Arawn indicated a muddy lay-by next to a dry stone wall with a small gate in it and said "Pull over and park here next to that gate. The rest of the way is on foot".

They all got out. Paul locked the vehicle while Arawn produced a key, unlocked the padlock and removed the hefty chain securing the gate. They walked through into a small wood. Arawn chained and locked the gate behind them.

There was a faint path winding its way between the trees. Arawn led the way. There were not many signs of regular use. Apart from the vague footpath, the place was an almost impenetrable tangle of brambles, gorse and trees. You probably wouldn't get any ramblers straying through here thought Paul.

Once she knew which way they were heading Izzy took the lead and trotted on ahead eager to sniff out any interesting smells.

"Not far" said Arawn from ahead. He continued for a few minutes and stopped in a small clearing next to a rock.

"Here we are" he said, breathing heavily from the walk.

"Where exactly is here?" Paul asked looking around, all he could see was trees, undergrowth and a large moss and lichen covered rock.

"Just a moment" Said Arawn, "Now, you have to swear not to reveal any of this to anyone, ever."

Paul looked around rather disappointedly.

"Well, to be honest, there isn't that much to reveal! But yes I promise" He exclaimed.

"Ok, hang on" said Arawn he leaned over the rock and placed his hand on a small flat area that was clear of moss and lichen. The rock under Arawn's hand started to glow gently.

"What the f…" Paul said. A low grinding noise arose followed by a section of the rock cracking along two vertical lines about four feet apart with a horizontal crack joining them at the top to form a doorway. The inner piece moved inwards and to the side almost silently.

Izzy and Paul both watched in awe. "Wow, impressive" he said. The dark hole gapped at them. Arawn took a step in and down, immediately soft light emanated from the walls at knee height above each step of a descending stone staircase.

He carried on and turning, he beckoned Paul to follow.

"It's safe, come on"

Paul and Izzy moved in and followed Arawn down at least five or six steps before a gentle grinding sound came from behind. Paul turned in alarm and made to ascend the stairs.

"Its fine." said Arawn "it's all automatic, it'll open again when we leave, don't panic" he smiled. "I did exactly the same when I first came here"

Turning, they carried on down.

After twenty or so steps they arrived in a large domed room. About twenty metres from left to right, twenty metres to the far wall and about five metres at the highest point. In front of them was a perfectly flat wall as if a partition had been built across the middle of a larger diameter dome cutting it in half, while the rest of the space followed the contours of the curved roof to meet the perfectly flat floor.

To the left there was a section of wall that had the barely discernible outline of what could be a door with another smaller square panel to the side midway up the wall.

There were decorations and embellishments everywhere, what Paul thought of as Celtic knots engraved or inlaid into the dark grey floor remarkably similar to the designs on the orb. Trees 'grew' up the walls, all of the decorations appeared to be made of untarnished silver. Scrolls adorned almost everything except the flat wall that bisected the room which was totally bare and uniformly blank. Overall the effect was quite beautiful. Someone had put a lot of effort into creating this space.

Paul looked around the room. It was almost perfect, no cracks or imperfections. Everything was so well made; he wondered what it was made of. It certainly wasn't concrete; in fact, he wasn't sure what material he was looking at.

"This is amazing" he said "is it only you that knows about this?" He asked

"There were others in the past," Arawn replied, looking a little sad. "But they've all passed away or moved away, taking the secret with them. I take it you've heard of Druids?" He asked

"Yes of course" he nodded and managed not to roll his eyes.

"Well, we are, or were, a sect or branch of the main Druid movement if you can call it that, formed, as far as we can tell, about 5000 years ago. There were only ever a handful of us, keeping and passing this secret down from parent to child over two hundred and forty generations. Bryn Celli Ddu the burial mound is about a hundred metres from here. The *regular druids* built it as a burial chamber to be close to the Cymwynasgar ("the Benevolent" in English) which is the Welsh name they gave to the visitors. The Aliens I spoke of last night."

"What?" replied Paul finding it difficult to keep the scepticism out of his voice?

"You're telling me that this place is over 5000 years old? It looks brand new. There's no water penetration, no dust, that's not possible!"

"Impossible or not that's the truth" said Arawn with a shrug of his shoulders.

Paul found it difficult to accept but thoughts crossed his mind. The orb had shown him a video of a place using technology that was not available anywhere on Earth as far as he knew. In that context this place wasn't so odd.

The orb... suddenly a strong feeling came over him and he reached into his pocket and withdrew the device. It was glowing again as it had when he first found it.

Both Arawn and Izzy's eyes were drawn to it.

"What is that?" Arawn said

"Something illogical, that made me travel here all the way from France on an impulse"

Suddenly things changed.

Chapter 4

The door-like outline at the side of the room became more defined and the square area illuminated red to form a panel that after several seconds turned green.

"This is amazing, nothing like this has ever happened before!" Arawn said

The flat wall at the far end of the room had changed as well, from being the same as the unadorned parts of the room to having a gentle background glow almost like a plasma TV when no device was connected.

Paul walked over to the small green panel "Looks like a door to me?" He said looking at Arawn. "What do you think? Drink me?" he grinned "I actually meant, press it?"

"Yes I got the reference Alice." said Arawn rolling his eyes "This is all new to me. I really don't know."

"What the heck?" said Paul "I've not driven all this way on a whim to get to this point just to stop and go home!"

He pressed the panel.

Paul's thoughts were confirmed, silently, a door slid backwards into the wall and then into a recess to the side revealing a dark room.

They entered, which triggered soft slightly bluish, but warm lights to come on as they had when they first entered the building or vault or whatever it was.

This was a more conventional square room with vertical and horizontal surfaces. All were covered with the same silver decorative scrolls, trees and Celtic knots as the other room

In the centre of the room were two of what Paul could only think of as dentists chairs. Next to each chair stood a metallic column about three feet tall with two jointed appendages attached near the top like arms. There was nothing else in the room. Paul felt the same sense of newness as in the other room. How was that possible if it was as old as Arawn claimed?

Come to think of it, how were the lights still working? After thousands of years... that's a hell of a good battery he thought.

"This is incredible" he said "How is all of this so new and clean and working after that length of time"

"I don't know, it's always been the same whenever I've visited." said Arawn "Which is usually about once a year", he added looking perplexed but excited as well.

Paul walked back into the main room

Izzy was wandering around sniffing everything. She paid particular attention to the blank wall and was walking backwards and forwards sniffing all the time. Not quite agitated but Paul knew her well and asked

"What is it Izz?"

She whined and continued her pacing back and forth across the front of the wall

"What's up with Izzy?" Even Arawn noticed.

"I'm not sure" said Paul "but it's not normal"

He walked towards her and stopped two feet from the wall. He peered at it closely

"It's odd. It's almost like it's not solid" he said slowly reaching out a hand he touched the wall. Or rather he didn't. His hand simply broke the surface of whatever it was and passed through. He couldn't actually see his hand; it was as if it passed through an invisible curtain.

"Shit!" He exclaimed and pulled his hand back quickly as if stung and then laughing at his own cowardice he moved away.

"What just happened?" Arawn said coming closer to Paul

"I'm not sure, but I think there might be another room here, or at least another doorway. How wide is it?"

He stood back to get a better view and noticed that indeed there was a slight difference in texture between a section about three metres square and the rest of the wall. He touched the other, different, part of the wall and it was solid. Coming back to the centre of the wall he touched it again and again his hand entered the surface and disappeared from view.

"Ha! What do we do now?" He muttered

"What do you mean we?" Arawn asked seriously, but grinning at the same time.

Paul laughed, breaking the tension.

"Well, so far all of this has been pretty benign? You mentioned the druids named them what?"

"Cymwynasgar, the Benevolent? Benevolents?" replied Arawn

"Yes … doesn't sound like an evil race to me? How about we step through and have a butchers?" He asked

"Well, I'm not sure that's such a good idea" Arawn said

"Ah come on, in for a penny?" Paul shrugged

He stood up straight, took a deep breath and walked towards the wall. He stepped through what felt like nothing until his rear foot left the ground in the room behind him then a weird feeling of dizziness like vertigo came over him just before his front foot touched solid ground and he was on the other side of the doorway.

Immediately lights came on revealing a room about the same size and almost identical to the one he'd stepped out of a moment before. It was empty except for what looked like a desk with a chair; a doorway was outlined in the wall opposite where the staircase was in the other room, almost a mirror image of the first room.

He turned around and looked at the wall again. This side seemed to be exactly like the other. He reached out and touched it. The same thing happened and his hand disappeared.

Ok he thought I need to make sure I can get back he laughed. Not that he could have done anything about it if he couldn't. So he stepped through, returning back to the room he'd just left. Izzy jumped on him whining and licking him as if he'd been gone ages. "Whoa it's ok sweetie I'm ok, I won't leave you"

"She was really worried when you disappeared" said Arawn "Actually I was a bit concerned too" he laughed. "What's in there?" He asked.

"Why don't you come and see? In fact let's all go."

"Ok" said Arawn appearing to grow a little in confidence.

Paul called Izzy and keeping her close urged her into a walk and stepped through the barrier. Arawn followed.

Arawn laughed "Well this is a bit of an anticlimax. Not really sure what I was expecting. It's an odd thing to do though, don't you think? "

"What is?" said Paul

"Well, why go to all the trouble of building a doorway you can't see or hear through but you can physically pass through, in the middle of a room?"

"Yes that is odd" agreed Paul

""There's nothing odd about it!" A disembodied voice said from all around them.

Both Paul and Arawn jumped and turned around trying to see who had spoken.

There was no one there; the room was empty apart from the desk and chair.

A moment of silence passed. "Hello? My name is Paul Arwyn, who am I speaking to?" Paul tried.

"You may address me as Maxsar" the masculine voice said in a not too pleasant manner.

"My name is Arawn. Where are you?" Arawn said

"I am here" replied the voice.

"No, I meant where 'are you' physically, I mean? We can't see you" Said Arawn

"I am currently at an altitude of one thousand of your Earth kilometres above said planet"

Paul and Arawn looked at each other, their mouths dropping open.

Paul recovered first "Hang on, that's an amazing comms system then. How can you see us and hear us? We are at least thirty feet underground in what appears to be a concrete bunker."

Maxsar sighed as if being bothered by a petulant child

"What would you know about 'comms' systems? No, don't answer that... First, you are no longer in the transport hub and second, I can see you and hear you through an extremely complicated, or at least it would appear complicated to the likes of you, system of sensors built throughout my body"

The humans looked at each other again.

"Bit rude" said Paul "I only wondered "

"Are you saying we are currently on an alien spaceship in orbit around Earth?"

"Yes! Give that man a prize! You have stepped through the event horizon of *a* passage point between a transport hub and the nearest Madden ship to the planet." said Maxsar testily.

"Who are the Madden?" Said Paul "and you said a transport hub singular as if there was more than one?"

"Yes, there are twelve hubs on your planet. The Madden are a race of technologically highly advanced people who are at war with the Tylvar."

"So can you not come out and meet us?" Paul asked

"I am not a being of flesh, I am Maxsar"

"Ah, you're a computer," said Paul.

"I am no simple computer, human" Maxsar said, sounding a little annoyed.

Arawn whispered to Paul "Perhaps winding up a computer that controls a spaceship in which we're standing isn't a good idea?"

Paul shrugged, he was a bit annoyed himself, at the pissy attitude of the computer, but ok, so probably not a good idea to be a dick and antagonise it further.

Izzy as usual had taken off, sniffing around.

"Oh my, you've brought a dog with you!" Maxsar sounded stunned.

"Yes this is Izzy" said Paul "she's part of the family"

"That is good." Maxsar said.

Arawn had wandered over to the desk-like structure and was looking at it. Paul followed.

There was what appeared to be a small palm reader on one side of the surface. Paul put his hand to it. It lit up white briefly then went out.

"Hmm" he said "can't win 'em all"

Arawn went to try it but Paul said "No point, obviously doesn't do anything"

Arawn ignored him and placed his hand on the plate. The same white glow appeared then turned green and the whole desk surface lit up like a Christmas tree.

"How the hell did that happen?" Paul exclaimed a little annoyed that Arawn had got it working when he couldn't.

"The magic touch" Arawn chuckled, waggling his fingers in the air.

"Magic. Ha! Trust you humans to think it's magic" Maxsar said disparagingly "it's a simple genetically coded reader. Mr. Arawn has the semi active gene but Mr. Paul's isn't active"

"What?" Both humans said almost together

With yet another heavy sigh, Maxsar spoke as if he was repeating the same thing for the fifteenth time today!

"How to dum this down sufficiently... All Madden technology, from the lowliest device to the most complex, is controlled or more accurately, accessed, by your genes. Or more accurately still, by a reading of the complete genome to identify who is attempting to access the device. This system was developed to try and prevent the Tylvar from using our technology. There are some other races, including yours, that are also recognised genetically."

"Merely being a member of one of the "other" races..."

Paul could hear the derogatory air quotes around "other"!

"...isn't necessarily enough to access and use Madden technology. You need certain genes to be active. And also have certain combinations of base pairs" Maxsar continued oblivious to the irritation his haughty tone was generating among his audience.

"Not only does it allow you to use Madden technology but certain gene activations have other effects."

"Whoa wait a mo" said Paul "so if I don't have the ability to operate anything here, then how come I could see the message from the orb and operate the door switch in the other room? And also how has it stopped my pain?"

"The "orb" as you call it gives certain user rights to the bearer and emits a localised pain dampening field designed, in the case of injury, to get the candidate to the destination where repairs can be carried out. Simple things deemed necessary to get you to this point but no further. It was decided that any simpleton should be able to use it"

"Now hold on a minute, who the fuck are you calling a simpleton! You arrogant twat!" Paul shouted.

Arawn was looking a little worried at the way events appeared to be unfolding and tried to intervene.

"You said Paul's genes were not active?" He said, changing the subject.

"Indeed." Replied Maxsar

"Can they be activated?" Paul picked up on Arawn's question.

"Yes, a simple procedure. That is what the secondary space in the vault is for."

"The dentist's chairs", thought Paul "Is it dangerous?" He asked

"Only to races who have not been catalogued "

"What does *being catalogued* involve?" He asked warily, not liking the sound of it at all.

"Nothing more than a tiny tissue sample"

"Oh ok. And does it hurt?"

"Why are you asking these questions?" asked Arawn. "You're not thinking of doing it are you?"

"Why wouldn't I?" Paul asked "you obviously have some of these enhanced genes already and it hasn't done any damage that I can see… apart from a taste for bad shirts perhaps!" Paul said referring to the different coloured lumberjack shirt Arawn had worn today

Arawn huffed and tried to disguise a smile by shrugging his shoulders and said "On your head be it!"

Paul asked again "does it hurt?"

"The procedure itself does not hurt. There may be a period of discomfort during the *adjustment* phase"

"That doesn't sound too bad. How long does it take?"

"The procedure itself, seconds. The *adjustment* can be anything from minutes to days. Everyone reacts differently."

"Hmm ok, how do i do this?" Paul asked

"Return to the adjustment room and we can begin" said Maxsar

Paul looked at Arawn and shrugged. "What the heck, why not, I've got nothing to lose"

He was totally stressed at this point bordering on hysteria. Things had moved so quickly he felt he might lose it at any moment. But his pilot training had given him the ability to assess extremely fast changing situations and make split second instinctive decisions vital for survival.

He sensed no danger from Maxsar other than a bit of an attitude towards the "other" races. Ha! A racist computer that's a new one he thought. No, he couldn't see any objections other than the usual… it's dangerous, it's scary, its life threatening you know, minor things like that.

Arawn shook his head but said no more.

Paul called Izzy over. They walked back through the portal, this time as if they'd been doing it all their lives.

Back in the 'other room', as Paul thought of it, or actually, back on Earth, he paused and looking at Izzy said "Can you really believe we've just travelled a thousand kilometres into space and back just like that? Amazing "

"One thousand and six point one two kilometres to be exact" piped up Maxsar.

"You're here as well?" Asked Paul

"Of course I am. Did I not mention the *magical* sensors I am equipped with?" Paul could almost hear Maxsar rolling his eyes.

"Doh! Yes, point taken."

Arawn laughed.

"What do I do?" Paul asked

"Take a seat on either couch"

Paul climbed onto the nearest.

"Settle back and try to relax" Maxsar said

Paul put his head on the headrest and closed his eyes, immediately getting uncomfortable flashbacks of previous visits to the dentist.

He heard a gentle hum, opened his eyes and turned his head towards the pillar next to the couch. One of the arms now had a rather large vial of clear liquid at the end of which was a gun type implement. It approached his head.

"Maxsar what's this?" He asked, panic edging into his voice.

"This is the serum that contains the gene therapy."

"Woah, you never said anything about a serum. That sounds like viruses and other dangerous stuff!"

"It's nothing to worry about. It is not a virus it's actually millions of pico nanites that alter your DNA at an atomic level rearranging the very chemical bases of your genes"

"Okay so not a virus but I'll have millions of tiny robots inside me? And that's better how?"

"They deactivate after completing their work and are excreted harmlessly out of your body."

"Hmm ok… let's do this then" but his voice couldn't hide his misgivings.

He lay back down and the arm approached his neck. It made gentle contact and hissed. Paul felt coldness in his neck that travelled upwards to his brain.

Suddenly he lost his sight, he felt a rising panic then blackness descended. He wasn't totally unconscious though; he felt a sudden pain in his right hand. He heard voices, all talking over each other. The panic threatened to overwhelm him but he fought back, trying to regain consciousness. His hearing suddenly returned and he could hear Izzy barking frantically. He managed to open his eyes and look around. Arawn stood next to him holding onto Pauls arm and leg as if trying to restrain him. Izzy was barking furiously and dancing around the couch in an agitated state.

"What the hell happened?" He muttered.

"You had a bad reaction to the serum" said Maxsar "and suffered a seizure" it only lasted a few seconds but I see you managed to break the equipment."

"Gee, thanks for caring more about the equipment!" said Paul. He examined his hand which must have struck the robotic arm. Although probably due to the effect of the orb, he didn't feel any pain anymore.

"Damage to this sensitive equipment takes time and energy to repair" Maxsar said sniffily.

Paul looked at Izzy and held his hands out to her. She sniffed and licked him delighted to see him back to normal.

"I'm ok kid no harm done"

"Hmm says you" said Maxsar

Paul surveyed the *damage*. The only thing he could see was the arm with the injector lying limply by the side of the pedestal the cracked vial leaking a gathering pool of liquid on the floor.

"That's not bad" he said.

"It takes an hour to produce that amount of serum" said Maxsar

"Oh really, *an hour*, whatever, it's not like we've got a queue!"

He waved around him then turned back to see Izzy lapping the serum off the floor.

"Izzy NO!" He yelled at her.

She dodged backwards away from the broken vial.

"Shit! Maxsar what will happen to Izzy?"

"I am not one hundred percent certain. The serum was never tested on dogs. I surmise if she survives the next few minutes I think she'll be fine"

"Surmise! think! You're a bloody computer, how can you not know? You've got this super dooper sensor system so use it!!"

"That would be an abuse of my abilities"

"DO IT! Or I'll start smashing things up here."

"Fine!" He sniffed. "Typical organic behaviour, but I will scan Izzy."

A few seconds passed.

"Well?" Said Paul

"Well what?" Said Maxsar

"Oh for fu… how is she?" He said, biting his tongue and rolling his eyes.

"Izzy is fine. No adverse reaction unlike you.

He knelt in front of Izzy cradling her face in his hands. He stared at her and said. "Sorry kid, you gave me a real shock. Please don't do anything like that again"

"*Ok*" he heard a voice say.

He looked at Arawn.

"What?" Arawn asked after a couple of seconds.

"I was talking to Izzy not you..."

"I didn't say anything!" Arawn said defensively

"Yes you did. I said don't do anything like that again, and you said Ok"

"No I didn't "

"You bloody did"

"No me!" The same voice again only this time Paul was looking directly at Arawn when he heard it.

 "Did you hear that" Paul asked.

"No I didn't hear anything"

Maxsar spoke "I think your question is directed at the wrong person" he said with a note of amusement.

"What does that mean?" Paul asked

"The serum is designed to enhance your genes but it also unlocks latent abilities like telepathy for one. There is only one other person in the room"

The penny was in the air... Paul turned to look at Izzy who was sitting calmly looking back at him.

"Izzy, can you hear my thoughts?" He formed the words in his mind but didn't speak.

"Yes dad. Is good"

Paul was speechless… he stood there his hand went to his forehead, his mouth moving up and down but no sound coming out. No amount of military training could prepare you for something like this.

Somewhere in Paul's subconscious a penny hit the floor.

"Oh my god." He said and plonked himself down on the couch.

Arawn was looking between the pair of them "Will you please tell me what's happened?"

"I can hear Izzy's thoughts and she can hear mine" said Paul.

"Oh is that all." Arawn said "…yeah right pull the other one"

"I'm serious… how to prove it?" He muttered.

"Izzy, can you smell what Arawn ate this morning?"

Izzy walked over to Arawn and sniffed him a few times.

"Bacon, like bacon "

"Yes I know you do" Paul thought back and smiled.

"Izzy says you had bacon for breakfast?"

"What? No, I, how could she know that?"

"She can smell it and she told me"

"Lucky guess" said Arawn.

"No it's true" said Maxsar. "As I said the main enhancement of the adjustment is telepathy. Seemingly it works on dogs too."

"How do you know? You're a computer" said Arawn, feeling a little left out.

"I am so much more than a computer, you Neanderthal. No, I take that back, Neanderthals were more intelligent. It's simple; I can detect and use telepathic energy."

Paul was sitting still, shell shocked from the latest revelation. It was incredible, fantastic even. He'd always felt a close link with Izzy since he first found her now they could talk to each other. Hold on he thought, bloody hell, I AM TELEPATHIC!!

Chapter 5

"This is too much to take in" said Paul feeling a sense of shock.

"I've got to get some air."

He turned and walked out of the treatment room and started walking up the steps when he thought *"come on Izzy"*. He didn't need to turn to look because an *"Ok"* appeared in his mind and he heard her claws on the steps.

As he neared the top he heard the door slide open and daylight came in.

They walked into the small clearing, if it could be called that, taking deep breaths and trying to relax, rolling his shoulders and shaking his head. Izzy seemed quite happy and sat there watching him.

"What's happening izz?" he thought

"It's good" she replied *"Izzy loves dad"*

That hit him hard. The emotional roller coaster of the last few months and especially the last few days had been incredible, frightening, confusing not knowing, not having a plan, a direction, a goal.

Then this… he could actually understand his dog and she could understand him. It was totally crazy.

Then it struck him like a bolt of lightning, the one real thing he could take strength from, probably the only thing that mattered, a solid foundation, it would ground him, the one thing that seemed to make it all ok was just so simple, Izzy had called him dad and she loved him.

"Ha!" He shouted, tears filling his eyes, he felt a new strength surging into him. He danced around the clearing, which wasn't a good idea because after two steps he tripped and fell. Izzy pounced on him, play fighting, Paul was laughing not hysterically but with joy mixed with relief.

They wrestled on the floor for nearly a minute laughing and growling until Izzy nipped a little bit too enthusiastically. "Ouch" Paul laughed, waving his hand around, more out of habit than need, because of the effects the orb had, the pain vanished after a couple of seconds.

They both sat panting on the floor for Paul, the emotional release felt good.

For Izzy she'd never had such a good time… *"Again!"* She thought

"Ha ha sorry Izz not just yet" Paul thought.

Izzy replied *"huh, ok"* sounding disappointed.

Arawn cleared his throat politely behind Paul. "Erm not to put a dampener on things but shouldn't we be talking to Maxsar?"

Paul sighed where he lay. He took a deep breath and blew it out. He knew what he wanted to do now; it was clear in his mind. He felt he had his feet back on solid ground.

He got up, said

"Come on, troops, time to find out what's going on!"

And walked confidently back down the steps into the passage point.

 Izzy and Arawn followed and the doorway closed behind them.

He marched towards the event horizon and straight through to the ship beyond.

"Right then Max! Tell me everything, but first can we get some more comfortable seats? I've a feeling we may be here for a while." he said

"Please, my name is Maxsar," he replied, still annoyed. "There are more comfortable quarters down the corridor and what exactly do you want to know?"

"Let's go and find somewhere we can sit and talk and can we get anything to eat or drink?" He said marching towards the only other door in the room.

Silently this door opened automatically as he approached.

He smiled and thought.

 "Another benefit of gene therapy?" He instinctively directed the thought towards Maxsar

"Yes, one of many." Maxsar replied "Interesting, I notice you managed to communicate with me without any difficulty? And I might add without shouting"

"So?" Paul flashed back.

"Most beings, new to the skill, have problems coping at first and it takes time to adjust and fine tune the ability. Have you ever had telepathic experiences before?"

"Not that I can recall?" He answered.

"Odd" said Maxsar in a way that implied he had filed the question away and the conversation was not finished.

"Max, now that Izzy can communicate telepathically, can you let her know what we are saying when we speak vocally? I think it would help"

"Of course, I will automatically re transmit to Izzy alone everything we all communicate verbally" she said.

The corridor outside was brighter than the grey of the portal room and had a lot less decoration. He could see numerous other doors to the left and the right. It was at least a hundred metres long, possibly longer, three wide and about two and a half high. Also, now he knew, he could feel a gentle hum all around like the feel of engines. We really are on a ship he thought

"Which way Max" He asked

"Follow the blue arrows" said Maxsar, still huffing at being abbreviated.

Paul smiled, he was beginning to enjoy winding Maxsar up.

After forty or fifty metres the arrows stopped at a door. There was a sign on the wall next to it. It resembled Earth style Roman script i.e. the letters were recognisable but not a language he could understand. "What's the sign say" Paul asked

"It says cafeteria in Madden" replied Maxsar

"Sounds promising" said Paul.

"I'm starving and I could murder a cup of tea" said Arawn

The door slid open and they walked in. The area was quite large; along one wall to the left were a bank of at least a dozen of what looked like vending machines.

But what truly and utterly amazed Paul and Arawn was straight ahead.

There were comfortable chairs and low tables, laid out among plants of various kinds, but behind them was the biggest single paned window they'd ever seen, completely filling the wall and there, glistening like a beautiful green blue and white marble was Earth….

"Oh my god" said Paul

"Look at that" said Arawn.

They stood still not saying a word for what seemed ages then turned to each other grinning and suddenly burst out laughing at the incongruity of the situation.

"Shit, they'll never believe this one at the pub!" Said Arawn and they both cracked up once more.

After a couple of minutes gazing out at the planet they turned back and took in the rest of the cafeteria.

Tables and chairs were arranged in rows covering most of the rest of the room.

It looked like any dining room in any business, school or military establishment anywhere on Earth apart from the view, which they kept turning to look at.

Paul said "Well, if nothing comes of this adventure then it was worth it just to see that "

"Totally" agreed Arawn

Izzy had taken off doing her usual sniffing of everything. She paid particular attention to the vending machines.

Looking down, Paul noticed that the furniture seemed to be fixed to, or possibly growing out of the floor.

"This," said Maxsar. "Is dining area one. The machines along the wall are designed to replicate any beverage and food item you might ever need. They are currently set to reproduce Madden dishes and drinks. They are biologically compatible with humans but may not be to your taste"

Paul asked "Is there anything Izzy can eat?"

"Yes, there is a dog menu"

"Really, you're joking?" Paul replied

"Dogs are revered by the Madden. Are you aware of the tales of the Mabi?"

"The Mabi?" Paul paused thinking "Do you mean the Mabinogion?" He was beginning to detect a common theme, ancient Welsh-Celtic myths and legends and it would seem the Madden were the source.

"It is possible that's what the name evolved into here on Earth. They contained references to a person called Arawn who was a Madden Lord? He visited Earth when the passage point was constructed. He had dogs and like Izzy they accompanied him everywhere."

"Well blimey looks like we're in good company Izz"

"Of course" she thought back. Paul smiled, he liked this telepathic link.

He wandered across to the replicators and looked at a screen. It was all in Madden. "I can't read Madden" he said

"Just touch the screen" said Maxsar.

Paul touched the screen and to his surprise the text turned to English. "Impressive" he smiled.

"Now, what shall I have? Hmm" The menu options were grouped into savoury, sweet, drinks etc. then submenus allowed him to select actual items. However, all the names were a *best translation* from Madden and still didn't make much sense.

"What is this stuff? I'd settle for just a sandwich and a coffee? Can you make them do that Max?"

"Same here that would do for me too" said Arawn who'd been studying another replicator but not really getting anywhere.

Maxsar said "Try these" and the replicator hummed into life, a hatch opened on both replicators revealing a plate with what looked like a cheese sandwich and a mug of steaming black liquid.

"Cool" said Paul picking up the items and putting them on a nearby table.

"*Izzy are you hungry*" he thought then to himself "*stupid question*"

"*Hungry, yes!!*" came back

"Can you rustle up something for Izzy please" asked Paul

More humming and the hatch opened to reveal a wonderful plate of meat, with what looked like vegetables and gravy.

"Wow, that's from the dog menu?" Paul asked looking at his slightly curly, maybe cheese, sandwich. "Oh well" he shrugged

He carried it all over to a table and sat down putting Izzy's food on the floor. She abandoned her "cataloguing" of Madden smells and came trotting over, took one sniff and suddenly was devouring it as if she'd never been fed before.

Paul and Arawn both laughed."Well, it's a big hit with someone" Arawn lifted the corner of his pale sandwich and looked at the *cheese*?

He took a bite, paused, then chewed and swallowed.

"I suppose you wouldn't starve" he took a sip of the "coffee" "hmm not bad almost but not quite coffee"

Paul started to eat his own, having waited to see Arawn's reaction.

"Hmm" he said "I might have to see what else is on the dog menu…"

Paul said "So Max, tell us your story. From the beginning"

"Are you certain? It will take almost four days and seven hours?"

Paul chuckled. "Ok, can you give us the edited highlights and if we want to know more we'll ask?"

"Very well"

And so Maxsar began

"The Madden are from Maeth a planet in this galaxy approximately ninety two thousand light years from Earth.

Several hundred thousand years ago the Madden developed a means of faster than light portals between two points anywhere in the known universe. The only limitation, the distance travelled was directly proportional to the input power. However, they had developed generators that could in theory draw almost limitless amounts of power from dark energy, the substance that binds the universe.

The limit was a practical one: to travel across the galaxy in one passage would require a power generator the size of a sun twenty times greater than Sol.

Using the energy to power the Passage Points they gradually, over millennia, created a network of passage points across the galaxy allowing travel across many light years almost instantaneously. They were created in areas away from planets and suns. The generators required are large satellites ranging from one to three kilometres in diameter. They have excellent cloaking abilities the same as this ship so they are pretty much invisible. The only way to find them is via a map and when within 1000 kilometres to activate the passage point by emitting a coded certain type of radiation.

Using these portals they could cross the whole galaxy. The fastest anyone has crossed all one hundred and twenty thousand light years is two years.

Paul whistled "That's impressive. And is there a portal near Earth?"

"Yes in fact there are three, located at in different parts of your system. The Madden are an enlightened race and developed certain skills such as telepathy. They felt these skills should be shared with other races and so began to take a benevolent interest in planets where intelligent space faring life might develop and, if required, give them the tools they would need to communicate with the Madden at some point in the future."

"These tools were designed to modify DNA as you experienced earlier. Two hundred and fifty thousand of your Earth years ago The Tylvor's ancestors were "visited" by the Madden. Two hundred thousand and seven years ago, It was Earth's turn."

"Around five thousand five hundred years ago, the Tylvor developed space flight."

"Isn't that what the Madden wanted?" asked Arawn?"

"Yes" said Maxsar

"However things began to go wrong a hundred years later or so…" Maxsar paused as if finding it difficult to continue.

"What happened?" Paul urged

"They found the passage points"

Maxsar stopped. "And…?" Paul made a carry on, rolling motion with his hand

"This is difficult for me to speak aloud. After all these years it feels like a confession… a few years later the Tylvor started conquering other worlds"

"This had never been The Madden's intention." Maxsar said a little too quickly, almost guiltily, if that was possible for a machine.

"It would appear that The Madden, we, had taken our eyes off the ball to use an Earth phrase."

"So, many years later the Madden decided to step in and try to "correct" their mistake and began fighting the Tylvor. But The Tylvor proved to be excellent fighters. Partly because of their evolution on a planet that had an extremely competitive and violent environment. It was populated with many aggressive and strong apex predators and given the Tylvor's own naturally aggressive nature they developed into fearsome enemies."

"The Madden unfortunately are scientists and artists, not warriors, and were slowly beaten back. The galaxy is a huge place and it took many hundreds of years for The Tylvor to cause the Madden serious problems. However, the Madden ruling council began to realise they were losing the war."

"Under the guidance and command of Lord Arawn, in a dwarf galaxy local to the Milky Way, I believe you refer to it as the Carina Dwarf Galaxy, four hundred thousand Light years away we discovered a solar system that had an abundance of metals and other precious elements so we set up remote autonomous factories to build dark energy powered ships and other military hardware that we and our allies could use."

"Don't tell me," said Paul "I've seen this movie. The Tylvor found out and took the lot? "

"Not to my knowledge" replied Maxsar "but unfortunately due to my own problems I am unable to confirm any of that. In fact I have been out of contact with my base of operations for quite some time."

"However, I do know the location is only accessible via a carefully concealed Super passage point.

"The super passage point is powered by a planet sized power generator. And it is designed to allow the passage of a supercarrier, the Dritan. I do know that if the fleet has not been discovered or used by the allies the autonomous factories were instructed to continue building weapons and ships until they ran out of raw materials. We realised it would take many hundreds of years to complete the task.".

"The weapons and other technologies available in these ships were far ahead of anything the Tylvor possessed at the time."

"The fleet required crews but the Madden were not especially good at fighting so the idea was to recruit the "junior races". The Junior races are those they had prepared or were about to prepare for contact over the previous thousands of years."

"Originally these *vaults* or outposts were built as bases for befriending the local populations but the Madden hierarchy realised that they had at their fingertips, an excellent means for recruiting soldiers, pilots etc. and due to the previous genetic seeding, that had the correct genes, that would allow them to use the equipment in the *Missing fleet*. The vault at Bryn Celli Ddu was one of the first created. The Druids didn't know anything about the portal but had a faint telepathic sense of it hence why they felt they should build the barrow where they did."

"Many years later, I was on the way here to commence recruitment, with my crew, when we were ambushed by two Tylvor ships. I was damaged, my core was corrupted and the life support was affected as part of the damage." Maxsar said this last bit slowly and stopped speaking.

After a few seconds Paul spoke "Oh damn, I'm sorry Maxsar…how long was the life support offline for?"

"About ten years "

"What? I don't understand" Asked Arawn

"The crew…" Paul said out of the side of his mouth.

"Oh! Yes, sorry" he said

"Did they suffer?" Asked Paul

"It was over in seconds." He said. "The maintenance systems took care of the bodies."

"Blimey. How many were there?"

"One hundred and six, not all crew, some were due to man the vault and try to recruit from among the locals."

Arawn laughed and tried to cover it up out of embarrassment at his terrible timing.

"What's so funny?" Asked Paul

"Well, just the thought of recruiting a bunch of Druids and subsistence farmers to man and fly a ship like this struck me as funny, sorry"

"It is a bit" Paul smiled. "So it took you many hundreds of years to get here flying sub light speed? What exactly is the damage you mentioned?"

"My memory core has been corrupted. My memories are built like ropes or strands; they can be cut or diverted. When that happens I can't get around the problem. This affects my ability to think and if the damage is in my base matrix, it's possible even my core programming could be compromised."

"Can you show us the problem?" Asked Arawn

"I can show Paul, telepathically. It's difficult to explain but the matrix was designed by telepaths and can be programmed or manipulated by them as well. Physical interaction, as happened in this case, can also cause problems."

"Let me see." said Paul.

"The only way is through the programming suite. It allows you to link into my matrix in a controlled environment. "

"Is it far?"

"Two decks up and in the central section" said Maxsar

"Let's go" said Paul. They had finished their refreshments so left the cafeteria with a final glance back out of the window.

Following another set of arrows on the floor, they came to a door which opened into a large lift.

Once everyone was on board the door closed and with hardly any feeling of acceleration it smoothly took them up two decks.

It was a good five minute brisk walk to reach the programming suite. The doors opened automatically and a dimly lit room with four comfortable looking chairs arranged in a semicircle with a control console in the centre.

Max said "Please sit in one of the chairs and attach the small pad to your temple."

Izzy had already made herself at home on one of the chairs making Paul smile.

He sat and found a tiny pad on a wire lying on one of the arms of the chair. He brought it up to his temple, when it was near enough it moved and attached itself with a very faint click.

"As there is no technician present I will initiate the sequence to enter the programming domain" said Maxsar

Gently the chair elongated and reclined. Paul felt his eyelids getting heavy and he fought to keep them open.

"Please don't fight the sensation" Maxsar said "it isn't sleep per se, you will be wide awake, but the system requires that you have no visual distractions."

Paul allowed his eyes to close.

Suddenly he felt as if he was travelling along a dark tunnel towards a light "oh shit, don't go towards the light!! Ah hah, hah, hah." he chuckled. But before he could do anything else he broke through into a bright almost infinite area of brightly coloured for want of a better word, tubes. There were thousands laid out below him, stretching as far as the eye could see, in many different colours, all laid out in parallel, and heading in the same direction pulsing randomly.

He gasped *"this is incredible. What am I seeing here Max?"*

"This is my main core. The different coloured chords are routines, sub routines and functions of my main programming, in essence, me"

"How do I move about?"

"Just think it, up, down, left, right etc."

Paul tried it he thought *"turn 180 degrees"* and turned almost instantaneously. He could see a small dark opening, above the plane of the tubes, through which he assumed he'd arrived.

He turned around and thought *"forwards"* he shot so far and so fast that when he turned around to view behind him the dark opening had disappeared. "Er Max, how do I leave here?"

"Simply think, Exit!"

"Ok thanks. Right where is the problem?" Paul asked

"If you will allow me to direct you?"

"Go ahead "

Paul felt, not actual acceleration as he was used to in his F35, but a virtual acceleration as a side effect of the landscape passing by below, which was very odd. Within seconds he knew he'd reached the problem area as it was very different. A dozen or so of the neat parallel tubes were in a big tangle; some were no longer pulsing and some at the far side of the problem were dark.

"Wow right, it looks bad. How do I do this? He asked.

"Can you imagine your hands moving and gripping the conduit? You can break them by pulling them apart. And join them by putting two open ends together. They will automatically splice if matched correctly."

"Ok I'll give it a go"

He studied the rat's nest of tangled conduits and after a while he thought he could see a pattern. He picked a yellow one that disappeared into the tangle and broke it. The side nearest to him continued to shine but a previously glowing conduit on the other side of the problem extinguished.

"Ha! good one" he thought.

He moved over to the far side of the blockage and picked up the newly extinguished conduit, braking this one he brought the two open ends together. As they approached each other they started to whirl around seeking each other out coming together with an audible click and the dark side lit up and the light raced away into the distance.

"Absolutely incredible" Paul thought and he picked another conduit. He carried on like this, breaking and splicing those he could easily identify.

After all the illuminated conduits had been untangled he was left with several in a knot that had light entering the knot but no matching one exiting. So he decided to break all the remaining conduits before and after the knot and lay them down on what he called the ground. Gravity seemed to work here or something that simulated gravity.

After completing the task it was a simple process of trial and error bringing random ends together and seeing if they automatically spliced. Not much later, the job was completed.

All of the random leftovers of conduit he'd cut off had dissolved away after a while leaving the area looking exactly like the rest of Maxsar's memory.

He took one last look around and thought *"Exit!"*

He opened his eyes to see Arawn and Izzy sat on the other seats having a nap!

"Charming" He said. Arawn jerked awake "Sorry, it was boring waiting for you, any joy?"

"I think so, Max?"

"Thank you Paul, I am fully functional again so now I HAVE NO NEED FOR YOU WEAK AND PUNY HUMANS… DIE… Mwah hah hah hah hah!"

Silence gripped the room. Seconds passed

"A hah hah hah, you should see the looks on your faces… priceless. Ah hah hah hah hah." Maxsar laughed.

"Oh very funny" Paul said as he tried to suppress a smile "big ha ha!"

"What a knob" said Arawn "I nearly shit myself. Not impressed"

"Well, I thought it was funny." said Max.

"Moving on…" said Paul "what are your plans Max?"

"To begin with, this ship needs a captain. You are eminently qualified?" He paused leaving the question open.

Paul was a little flustered "I'm not a starship captain! I'm just a former fighter pilot. How could I possibly command a starship?"

"Well who else will? Izzy?" Max asked.

"Ok let me think about it. In the meantime we need to find out what's happening out there" he said pointing upwards. "It's been quite a while since you got any updates."

"Indeed. I have been giving it some thought since my full processing power was restored and I think the best way would be to try and contact some of the remote Madden outposts further out in the Orion spiral arm."

"If there are any Madden there they could relieve you of the captaincy and I could return you to Earth "

"Ok sounds like a plan a couple of things first. We have got to get the replicators working. Anything would be better than the last offerings. It's not quite haute cuisine Max" he said "can we alter the replicators in any way?"

"You would need to bring samples of food and place them in the replicator which could then reproduce the items entered. Simple."

"That could take forever" said Arawn laughing. He paused and thought more about it "Ooh Yes bacon rolls, fish and chips, ooh curry!" beginning to warm up to the idea.

"Beer, tea, coffee etc anything we can get hold of really. How large a sample do we need?" Paul asked

"Less than a gram but if it's a complex dish then I would suggest at least 20 grams."

"Ok Arawn can you do that? It's going to cost us though. Is there anything you can do to help Max?"

"If you return to the cafeteria we can prepare."

They made their way back and Maxsar directed them to the first replicator. The hatch opened and there were two neatly stacked and wrapped bundles of twenty pound notes and next to each one a debit card from a well known British bank made out in their names.

"Bloody hell" Paul said, shocked. "Are they real? Are we going to get arrested for fraud?"

"No. They are genuine cards and the account details are made out to match both of you exactly. I have created a bit of a back story for you both. I wasn't sure exactly how much you would need so there is one hundred thousand pounds in each account "

Silence greeted this last statement.

"Is that not enough?" Maxsar asked

"Err no! Its fine, fine" said Paul staring at the card and whistling softly.

Arawn was just grinning. "I've won the bloody lottery!" He whispered

"It is only to be used for legitimate expenses." said Maxsar

"Of course!" They both nodded in agreement.

"This all presupposes that both Arawn and I are going to come along with you?" Paul said

"Ah yes I haven't actually asked you as such have I?" Maxsar said sheepishly.

"No, there are a few things to consider. How long are we likely to be away? Does Arawn have family or other commitments? I'm ok all I have is here with me" he said looking at Izzy.

Arawn stared at his hands for a moment then looked up "I'm ok really; the only tie I have is my gran, who is in a home, as she has dementia. She doesn't really know who I am anymore. How long do you think we will be away Max?"

"Possibly four, maybe five?"

"Months?" Asked Paul

"No, weeks" said Maxsar

"That's not bad. And you think that'll give us enough time to do what we need?"

"Should do yes"

"Ok count me in" said Arawn

"Yes me too, Maxsar" said Paul

"Excellent, and what about the captain's position?" asked Maxsar.

"Ok, temporarily, only until I am relieved by a proper Madden starship captain"

"Of course." said Maxsar.

Chapter 6

"So Arawn, are you good to organise the food and any other supplies you might think we humans will need?" asked Paul

"No problem"

"Good let's get to it then. Here're the keys to the Land Rover" Paul said, throwing them over to him.

Arawn took his pile of cash and the debit card. There was a piece of paper attached with a PIN number. He looked at it, chuckled and made his way back to Earth.

Paul sat and thought. Should he let Louise know? Of course she wouldn't believe him, but she was the closest thing he had to next of kin. Perhaps she would be concerned if he disappeared? Then again she had left him, so maybe not. He didn't know.

An email perhaps... He opened the email app on his phone and started to type. He said he would be out of the country trying to get clean and wouldn't be back for a few weeks possibly longer. Hope she was ok and signed it with a kiss. He pressed send and lo and behold it actually went. He laughed.

"Hey Max, are we connected to the Earth internet up here?"

"Of course," Max said. "Easy as pie?" is that the correct expression?"

"Yes if you were one of our American cousins. A British expression would be a piece of cake, easy peasy or as easy as falling off a log?" Paul laughed and thought this trip might be good fun.

"Is there anything you or I need to do for the captainship? Any hand over or such like. I know there are customs observed by the Navy when doing so."

"Not really, merely stating loudly and clearly so it is recorded in the log "I accept the captaincy" should suffice." Max replied.

"Ok then. Maxsar, I accept the captaincy of the... what exactly is the ship's name Max?"

"Maxsar," he said.

"Sorry" said Paul "Look, I prefer short names or nicknames, but if you insist I'll call you Maxsar instead of Max. Although to be honest I did enjoy winding you up a little." he chuckled.

"No, you misunderstand, the ship's name is Maxsar and I have grown used to you calling me Max." Max replied.

"Oh, I see right. Well In that case I, Paul Myrddin ap Arwyn, accept captaincy of the ship Maxsar. Do I need to state a date or anything?"

Max was silent.

"Max? Hello?"

"Did you say your name was Myrddin?" max asked

"Yeeess? Why?" said Paul, a little warily?

"Are you aware of the legend of Myrddin?"

"Of course... Everyone in the UK knows about King Arthur and the Knights of the Round Table. Why? You're not going to say you knew him now are you?" Paul laughed.

"Yes, I did" Max replied

"Now you are joking. You knew Merlin and King Arthur?"

"They weren't humans. They were Madden lords who also visited Earth with Arawn. Myrddin and Artur were unusual Madden. They possessed other special skills. They both had the power of telekinesis and used it when building the vault you found. Arawn, Myrddin and Artur," Max pronounced Arthur in the French way with a "t" sound instead of the English "th."

"All three were part of a unique team travelling the stars, building the vaults."

"How the myths and legends grew and altered after they left? I can't say. But certainly they would have appeared to the locals as special people, possibly magical. Tribal memory is quite strong."

"Blimey," Paul said, surprised yet again by one of Maxsar's revelations. "I don't think I have anything to do with Merlin or King Arthur. My mum named me, and I think she was just a bit of a "new age" hippy type that liked the myth surrounding the name."

In fact Paul was totally unaware, but his mother *was* sort of a hippy, but had named him for a very different reason. Around the age of 1 year, Paul had a favourite soft toy dog called "doggie" and wouldn't sleep without it. If he ever lost it while asleep he would wake up crying. At first his mum would wake and give it back to him, but over time she took longer to react.

One night Paul woke her up crying, she looked over to the cot, saw that Paul must have thrown "doggie" out of reach to the bottom of the bed, laying back, exhausted, she drifted off, and awoke with a start, but this time Paul wasn't crying. She looked over at him and saw he was holding "doggie" again? There was no way Paul could have sat up, reached down to the end of the cot, picked up "doggie" then, got back into bed, dragged the blankets over himself *and* tucked them in, weird!

She went back to sleep. In the morning, she thought about what had happened and dismissed it as a trick of a very tired mind. Nothing more happened for another couple of days. She was in the kitchen and she heard Paul shouting, he had just begun to speak his first couple of words, "mum", and "oggie." He was shouting for "doggie." She walked into the living room where Paul was playing on the floor just as she saw "doggie" moving along the carpet and into Paul's outstretched hand. She stood shocked, her hand on her mouth. "No way" she exclaimed.

Many weeks passed and Paul progressed as any other baby would. There were no more "incidents." But Paul's mum never forgot the "magic" as she liked to think of it. She never told anyone else.

She wanted to mark it in some special way and decided that she would give Paul a middle name and settled on Myrddin.

Paul was oblivious to all of this of course. And grew up proud of his name apart from during his teenage years, when he tried desperately to keep his middle name a secret from mocking peers.

Sadly his parents died in a car accident when he was twenty two and the "anyone else" his mother hadn't told, included him.

"Named after a powerful Alien Lord!" he said. "Cool. It'd be nice if I had telekinesis as well." He joked.

"Hmm" max replied as if deep in thought.

"Is there some sort of bridge, or control centre on board?" asked Paul.

"Of course, just follow the arrows." Max said.

Paul followed the arrows back to the elevator they'd used earlier. This time it went downwards.

"I would have thought the bridge would be at the top of the ship?" He asked as they travelled.

"No, the safest area is in the centre of the ship. It has special hardened armour surrounding the bridge and it also contains my core. The bridge is designed to be a self contained ship in its own right. It is equipped with minimal life support, engines, sensors, a rail gun, point defence lasers and comms. In the event of the ship being too badly damaged it can eject and continue under its own power."

"Cool. What about the rest of the ship? Sounds a bit selfish if just the bridge can escape?"

"Not so, the ship contains escape pods for all of the crew in all of the key sections. So they too have escape routes."

The elevator stopped and Paul stepped out. The arrows flashed to a point directly opposite. He walked towards the door he could see, which opened for him as normal, except this door must have been a metre thick. It slid backwards just over a metre then sideways into the wall. Paul stepped through.

He was gobsmacked. The room was everything he'd imagined a spaceship bridge to be. A large comfortable looking command chair was in the centre of the room. In front of and facing away from the main command chair, arranged in a semicircle were four other chairs and consoles or at least he assumed they would be, because at the moment they just looked like the blank desk they had encountered in the transit room. The one he had failed to operate but Arawn had.

In front of the semicircle of consoles was a large curving blank wall. To the left Paul recognised a smaller version of one of the replicators they'd used in the cafeteria.

As per the cafeteria all of the consoles and chairs appeared to be melded into the body of the ship.

Izzy conducted her, by now usual "tour" of the place

"Max, the furniture on board, is it bonded to the floor?"

"No, all of the furniture on board and any other fixtures and fittings are organically "grown". This is essential in the event of gravitational forces being exerted that the dampening fields cannot cope with."

"That is amazing." Paul said truly awed.

"So, is this the captain's seat?" He asked pointing to what certainly looked like a command chair

"Indeed." said Max "Please take a seat Captain"

Paul sat and immediately the chair adjusted itself to his contours. It felt like leather but warmer and more comfortable.

A simple joystick appeared out of the arm on his right hand side almost identical to the controls in his F35 Lightning II. He smiled he actually began to feel a little more at home.

"All of the controls can be customised. You can move them either side of the seat. Try it, simply think it." Max suggested

Paul thought *"Joystick left"*. The joystick on the right melted back into the seat arm and reappeared out of the left hand arm.

"That is awesome." He laughed.

"Joystick right," he thought. And it appeared back on the right hand side.

"Is there a throttle control? Weapons?" he asked.

"Hold on, no don't answer that."

He experimented again with *"Weapons control left,"* he thought.

A pad appeared on the left hand arm of the chair and immediately illuminated. It had a touch screen with a single menu heading "Weapons" in English.

He touched the menu and it opened further sub menus: Rail Gun, Point defence rail gun, Point defence laser, Missiles, Plasma cannon.

"Shields" he thought, why not if all those movies had 'em…

Another smaller panel appeared in front of the weapons control panel. It simply showed the current status, one hundred percent, in green, there was a recharge time showing below of two minutes and a shape, which he took to be the outline of the ship with a green line all of the way around it. OK makes sense, he thought nodding.

"Throttle left" he thought.

A T shaped lever appeared. The previous two panels moved forwards and angled upwards and outwards for clarity. The lever was in the ideal position for Paul to use and still reach and see the other panels.

"Normally the captain wouldn't fire the weapons himself." suggested Max.

"Any of the consoles in front of you can be designated as weapons control. The consoles provide a greater degree of control and aiming as well. As the captain and pilot you will generally be otherwise occupied."

"Understood, makes sense." Paul replied. "Unfortunately if it's just me, I might need to do everything?"

Max suggested, "Arawn is quite capable of being shown how to use the weapons systems. In fact most of the functions such as aiming and reloading are controlled by a subroutine of mine. However in emergencies they can be manually overridden from the appropriate console and controlled by the weapons officer."

"Good idea we'll put it to him when he returns. Can I take her for a spin?" He asked coyly like a child asking for another biscuit they knew they weren't allowed.

"Of course, you are the captain." Max replied.

"Yes!" Paul said, punching the air. "I Like this. Has Arawn left the ship?" he asked.

"Indeed he left a while ago and has left the vault also"

"Talking of which what happens in the vault if we aren't here?"

"The range of that particular Passage Point is about ten thousand kilometres. But if we are moving or are out of range, there can be no connection and the event horizon remains solid"

"Ok how long has it been since Arawn left?"

"Approximately forty five minutes" Max replied. Paul wondered, "Can we track him?"

"Yes." Max replied.

The curved wall in front of the consoles suddenly lit up. It showed a map type view of Anglesey and the mainland. A small green flashing dot with a tag showing "Arawn" was in Bangor and he was walking through the car park of Morrison's supermarket. Several other amber dots were moving around him.

"Fantastic." Paul exclaimed. "This is amazing. I take it the other amber dots are other people and possibly vehicles?"

"Yes, anything or anyone not recognised and could be a possible threat is automatically marked as amber." Max said. "Anything positively identified as a threat is marked in red. All friendlies are marked in green."

Paul tried experimenting again. *"Sensors view space in front"* The viewing wall immediately went dark, almost dark. Paul suddenly realised what he was seeing. It was space with all the myriad stars shining as perfect white dots undistorted by the earth's atmosphere.

"Beautiful." He said. "Right then, *let's kick the tyres and light the fires*" he laughed uproariously.

"Is that some kind of Earth saying?" Max asked.

"Sort of" He laughed again. "We need to watch some movies."

He took the Joystick in his right hand and the throttle in the left. Slowly he eased the throttle forwards. A rumble started behind him somewhere in the ship and the stars began to move towards him. *"Show earth relative to us"* he thought. Earth appeared on the left hand side of the viewing wall and began to shrink rapidly. For the first time he noticed telemetry at the bottom of the wall showing speed, shields and weapons.

The speed display was showing 100 kilometres per second. He moved the stick further forwards, more boldly this time. The rumble from the ship increased, speed was now nearly 400 kps.

"Er, max? How fast can we go?"

"Theoretically 0.9c or approximately 270,000 kilometres per second. The maximum acceleration is 1000 earth gravities. It would take approximately 7.6 of your Earth hours to get to that velocity."

"One thousand gee's? My god, why am I not splattered over the back of this chair?"

"We have anti gravity systems on board that negate the effect of acceleration. They also work during combat."

"Hold on to something." He shouted. He moved the joystick control and the view turned as he spun and moved the ship in space.

"Max, can I VIF?"

"I'm sorry I am not familiar with this term." Max replied

"VIFing means altering the vector of the thrust from the engines while flying along in a straight line it stands for Vectoring in Flight."

"Ah yes I see. As well as the main engines you can use the thrusters which are positioned all around the ship to provide movement in almost any direction. Think thrusters and a direction. Direction is given in two dimensions: azimuth and elevation. For elevation, anything negative is below the ship, positive is above the ship."

Paul thought *"Thrusters 90 plus 90"* The ship began to move off at 90 degrees to the right and upwards at the same time.

"Woohoo! Awesome!" Paul shouted.

He thought *"Current position relative to Earth"* He then had an idea *"3D"*

The screen in front remained the same but a 3 dimensional holographic display appeared in front of the command chair showing the solar system.

"This just gets better." Paul said

A green dot representing the Maxsar was flashing and moving at a noticeable speed, even given the scale of the display, away from the plane of the ecliptic somewhere near Mars' orbit. They'd only been travelling for a few minutes. He could see all of the planets, the moons; he could even see some asteroids floating around. It was mind blowing.

Paul slowed down a little and turned the ship around. He pointed it back to Earth.

"Is there an Autopilot Max?"

"Yes I am fully capable of flying the ship."

"If that's the case why do you need a captain and a crew?"

"There are decisions I am not allowed to make such as firing of weapons and the manning of the vaults. Also I am not allowed to communicate directly with any of the "other races".

"How come you spoke to us then?"

"You were on board by that point."

"Ah yes, I understand. Ok can you pilot us back to where we were parked please?"

"If you mean can I place us in geostationary orbit, then yes"

"That's what I said." said Paul rolling his eyes.

"Are there any private quarters on board?" Paul asked.

"Yes there are crew quarters for all. The captain's bunk is just outside the bridge to the left."

"Let's go and have a look then."

He walked out, Izzy trailing behind.

He turned left and saw another door. This time the sign said *Captains quarters*.

"The signs have changed" Paul noted.

"Yes as you are now the official captain everything on board is now in your language by default."

"Never ceases to amaze..." Paul said laughing. The door to his quarters opened and he and Izzy entered.

They walked into a reasonably large reception come living room equipped on one wall with a sofa in front of which were a couple of arm chairs and a coffee table. Hidden lights illuminated the room in a comfortable way and highlighted art on the walls. Again, the same Celtic theme persisted. He didn't dislike it but perhaps something else to break the monotony anything really... dogs playing poker maybe? He grinned to himself.

At the opposite side of the room to the sofa a desk, or a console he should say, and chair and another curved wall, or as he now realised it was a view screen. *"screen on"* he thought. The screen turned on. It was currently set to duplicate the main screen on the bridge. It showed the Maxsar's current position, velocity, and various other critical bits of information.

"Are there any entertainment facilities on board?" he asked

"Yes, the Madden enjoy keeping fit, there is a gymnasium similar to Earth gymnasia. You can watch holos if you wish. When we are in the vicinity of a planet that has visual or audio transmissions we can pick them up and show on the display"

"Holos?" asked Paul

"Yes, recorded fictitious or factual dramatic events or enactments."

"We call them movies or films" Paul chuckled. That reminded him.

"Can you get copies of human movies and music from Earth?"

"Indeed, I have already downloaded many different cultural records and they are available to peruse at any time. Simply think what you want to see."

"Wow..." Paul was speechless.

He noticed another door opposite the entrance and walked over, it opened to reveal a bedroom with a large bed and continental quilt type covers. He thought that perhaps the Madden would 'do' sleep differently? But then again as they were humanoid, like Paul, would things be that different? They had similar nutritional and physical requirements.

There was a second door to the right it opened to reveal a bathroom. Not big but comfortable and further confirmation of the commonalities of humanoid species. There was a toilet, or at least a pedestal that could be a toilet.

In the corner was a shower cubicle and next to it a sink with a mirror.

All together it was as good as any hotel he'd stayed in.

"Max, just checking but is that a toilet? By that I mean a place for human waste, excretions?

"Indeed Madden and humans are quite similar in many ways."

"Yes I was beginning to get that impression. This will do very nicely he smiled."

"So, what else does the Maxsar have?" Paul asked as they returned to the bridge.

"We have two shuttle craft that can carry up to forty eight people and cargo. Four, of what you call fighters? They are small, single seat, armed and very manoeuvrable craft. They can also be used in atmosphere. They are capable of 800kps in space and 100kps in atmosphere and 1200 gees acceleration. They have excellent scanners, two missiles and two point defence lasers."

"Are the shuttles and fighters stealthy?" asked Paul "I mean are they invisible?"

"Yes. They have almost identical technology to the Maxsar. They have shields, they are invisible to your radar and active scanners up to a certain extent and they can deflect light around them. So to Earth technology and humans yes they are invisible."

"We could do with these in the RAF" he laughed.

"I am sorry but at the current level of technology Earth could not be allowed to possess these craft."

"I was joking Max."

"I see."

"Can I see these craft please?"

"Certainly, they are in their own hangars one either side of the ship. Follow the arrows."

Paul and Izzy followed the arrows out of the bridge and down the corridor past his quarters to another elevator at the end. He got in and was surprised this time the cab seemed to move sideways. "Is this lift moving sideways?" He asked

"Yes some are vertical only, and others can move in both directions."

The trip was short. Paul got out and carried on following the arrows. A thought occurred to him

"Max, do you have an image?"

"What do you mean?" Max replied.

"A form, a shape, what do you look like? Perhaps as a Madden or any other species, whatever takes your fancy I suppose and could you project the image as a convincing hologram?"

"I have never been asked that question before. That is an interesting idea. In theory there would be no problem technologically projecting an image anywhere in the ship. The only difficulty I would have is that an image, a persona has never been assigned to a ships Intelligence I am not sure morally and ethically if the Madden would accept it."

"Well the Madden aren't here at the moment and I am fed up of talking to the ceiling or thin air! Chose an image you are comfortable with and project it to follow me around please."

"It may take a moment." He said

"Ok we've got time."

Paul and Izzy carried on walking and they eventually reached a larger door or rather two doors as this was split in half vertically. They both swished aside as he approached and they walked into a hangar.

It was massive far bigger than the normal RAF hangars. There were two huge craft inside hooked up to large umbilical's hanging from the roof. They must have been at least a hundred metres long and fifty to sixty metres wide by twenty high. At the front was a glass window about 5 metres wide by a metre high presumably the cockpit. It sat on four massive legs and its belly was at least two metres clear of the floor.

Izzy thought *"Ball!"*

Paul laughed *"Yes I agree this is perfect for a game of ball. Unfortunately I haven't got it with me"*

"Oh..." She sounded so disappointed.

Paul reminded himself to make sure they had some quality time soon.

At the rear a ramp was extended down to ground level. Curious, Paul walked around to the rear and looked inside. The compartment had space for lots of cargo and up towards the front, rows of bucket seats for passengers. In front of them was a short ladder going to a hatch above presumably the cockpit.

"It looks good." Paul said aloud.

"Yes" said a voice from behind him. He jumped a mile...

"Jesus, who the hell are you?" He asked. Not knowing how dangerous this person might be, he looked around for anything he could arm himself with.

"It's me, Max!" the person said.

"What?" Paul laughed aloud. "Well you could have given me a warning before sneaking up on me like that."

"What do you think?" Max asked turning around.

"Is this what the Madden look like?" Paul said. "And is this particular image male or female because I am, how can I phrase this, seeing certain curves?"

"Oh I see, yes, this is a female form" said Max in his usual masculine voice.

"And you are happy with the choice you have made?"

"Yes very." She said.

"In that case you might want to adjust your voice a little because up until now I had thought of you as male."

"How does this sound." Max said having adjusted it.

"Better, a lot more feminine. This is very strange, how someone can change sex instantly like that. If it were real, there would be so many people queuing up for it on Earth!"

"Is Max still acceptable as your name? I guess it can be either masculine or feminine."

"Max is fine" Max said.

Oh well, Paul smiled to himself, of all the amazing things that's happened to me in the last few days what's one more?

He turned to his new companion and had a proper look. Max was tall and slim with, if she were human, a very attractive and athletic figure. She had short blond hair and piercing blue eyes. Her ears were slightly longer in an elfin way and she had a very nice smile. She wore a blue gray one piece suit with matching coloured boots. A belt around the waste and a name tag on the left breast that said "MAX"

"Can we have look at the fighters now he asked." He was trying to look at Max straight in the eyes.

"Of course" She said. "This way"

She pointed and led him across the hangar. He tried not to look, but finally admitted to himself, yes very athletic. He immediately felt guilty and admonished himself. She's an AI for goodness sake! Grow up!

They walked for about ten minutes from hangar one to hangar two. The same type of doors opened to reveal four magnificent looking fighters neatly lined up. All hooked to the umbilical's as were the shuttles. They looked immaculate, as if they'd never been used, fresh out of the factory.

"How do you keep everything looking so clean and in such excellent condition?" He asked as they walked to the nearest fighter.

"We use automatic bots and pico nanites. The same type of pico nanites you experienced. They can repair at atomic levels and the bots are used for larger jobs such as cleaning and moving large heavy items around." Max replied.

"They are constantly in operation even though you can't see it." She said.

Paul approached the fighter and climbed the ladder to look into the cockpit. The layout was so familiar to him he jumped in and touched the main screen in front of him. It came to life; all of the menus were in English. He quickly ran through a few. It seemed so straightforward. He felt he could take off right now and go and fly a mission. But as this was just a tour the mission could come later.

"I am so impressed with all of this Max" He turned and smiled down at her. She smiled back and said. "Come with me, there is one more place I think I should take you."

"Ok" he said a little mystified.

He called Izzy who was some way away and she came running over. They walked out of the hangar and got into a lift in the corridor. This time it went up. It stopped and they exited, Max turned left and Paul followed.

Paul thought how much better it was talking to another person rather than a disembodied voice even if that person was a hologram, albeit a very realistic hologram.

The sign on the door said Medical bay.

"Why are we here?" Paul asked

"You are currently not experiencing any pain are you?" Max stated.

"Correct, the orb sees to that" Paul said

"Indeed. If you were to lose the orb, or forget it what would you do, how would you cope?"

"Blimey yes I would be a wreck. I couldn't function even with all of the opiates I was taking. Damn, I don't want to go back to that."

"I thought not. We have very advanced medical facilities that should be able to treat your injuries in a matter of minutes and painlessly too. Do you want to make use of them?" She asked looking directly at Paul.

He had been so used to his injuries and finally a moment had arrived when he could be pain free again and depending how good the treatment was, possibly as good as new?

Still he hesitated. "What am I hesitating for" he thought. This is daft.

"Yes." He said "I'm in."

"Good" she said "follow me."

They walked into the medical bay which consisted of five couches laid in a row. Each had similar metallic columns to those they had found in the side room back on earth. These columns had four appendages each and were bigger.

The couches seemed bigger and more comfortable than the 'dentist's chairs' he'd sat on before. They also had flashing lights on them.

"Are the couches technological as well?" he asked.

"Yes they can scan your body and carry out some procedures themselves."

"Incredible" he said.

"Please hop on the couch and lie still" Max said.

He got onto the nearest. It immediately sprung to life. Elongating and reclining. He could see a band of light on the couch illuminate and begin to move along his body.

He chuckled. "I feel like I'm being photocopied!"

"What is photocopied?" Max asked.

"Just some Earth tech that copies a paper document and reproduces an identical copy" He replied

"Oh no, you aren't being cloned" she said.

"You can do that?" Paul asked

"Yes but that technology was banned millennia ago across the whole of Madden space. It caused some serious in-fighting and is a chapter in Madden history we all want to forget. The couch has completed its scans and diagnosis and is ready to begin the treatment. There will be no pain but it may feel uncomfortable. Are you ready?"

"Yes go ahead" Paul said.

The machine began to hum and he felt warmth in his back. His leg where the pins and plates were inserted also began to tingle. Suddenly the tingling in his leg began to move from what felt like deep inside near the bone he could feel movement it itched. He wanted to scratch it and began to move.

"It is important to keep still." Max said. "The removal of the metallic objects within your leg could damage blood vessels which, while not serious could be painful."

Paul sat still trying to ignore the itch. It had moved to the outer reaches of his thigh now and he could touch the area with his hand. Suddenly he felt something under his trousers. A hard object and it was growing.

"What the hell" he thought. It grew a bit more then seemed to fall out of his leg. He felt it through the material and it felt like a screw! Then he felt another, this time a larger, flatter item appeared and followed the others into his trouser leg. After a minute during which a total of six items had materialised out of his thigh it stopped. The tingling vanished. Meanwhile the warmth in his back had subsided also.

"You can get up now" Max said smiling "The procedure has completed"

He got up gingerly and stood. A tinkling noise came from his feet he looked down to see a collection of metal objects and screws.

He laughed. He bent at the knees and walked around the couch. He didn't feel any pain or discomfort. Then he remembered the orb. He fished it out of his pocket and walked to the far end of the room. He put it on the floor and slowly returned to Max twisting his body from side to side and taking large lunging strides to test his thigh.

He stopped and turned to face the other end of the room. He could see the orb where he'd left it it must be at least fifteen metres away. He'd never been this far away before. Previously anything beyond three or four metres and the pain would return. I'm actually cured. The emotions running through him caught him unawares and tears flowed down his cheeks.

"Dad good" Izzy thought looking up at him with pure love in her eyes.

"Yes dad good." He replied and cried even more.

A minute later he finally composed himself, he turned to Max and looked into her eyes. "Thank you, Max. I don't know what else to say just thank you."

She smiled and said "You are most welcome captain"

A thought occurred to him. "My addiction to painkillers, can anything be done about that?"

"Oh that was cured as part of the treatment. Also a small tumour was removed in your colon. It was not dangerous but standard procedure requires its removal automatically."

"You can cure cancer?" Paul gasped. "How long do madden live for?" It dawned on him given this kind of medical care life expectancy would be high.

"Yes we can. With careful and regular checkups the average Madden can live up to two hundred and fifty of your Earth years."

"Two hundred and fif..." Paul trailed off staggered.

"This treatment will have added ten years to your life. Subsequent treatments will enhance it further."

"Wow." Was all he could say.

Paul bent over to stroke Izzy. His mind was in a whirl. But his training kicked in and he focused on the present, on the mission.

"How long ago did Arawn leave?" he asked.

"Approximately 4 hours has passed."

"Is that all? Have we arrived back in orbit?

"Yes about fifteen minutes ago. Arawn is approaching the lay by in your vehicle. I would suggest he has many items to unload. Perhaps you should assist him" max suggested.

"Yes good idea. Is there any way I can talk to him? Can you tweak our phones at all?" he asked.

There was a very brief pause. "That is done" she replied almost instantly.

"Brilliant, thanks." Paul took his phone out and looked at the main screen there was an icon with the word MAX underneath and another with ARAWN underneath.

He tapped ARAWN and it rang almost immediately.

"Hello who's this?" he answered.

"The eye in the sky!" laughed Paul.

"Oh it's you. How did you get my... Max!"

"Yes, Max. You should have an icon to contact both of us on your main screen now as well. I am returning to the vault so I'll see you in a few minutes?"

"Great I could do with some help. See you in a mo" and he signed off.

"Let's go." said Paul.

Paul, Izzy and Max walked out of the medical bay and down the corridor. Paul suddenly for no reason whatsoever other than he hadn't done it in a long time broke into a jog. This turned into a run and eventually into a sprint. Max, was surprised but kept up, Izzy loved it and ran alongside Paul tongue lolling out and barking happily.

They got to the lift and Paul bent over gasping for breath and laughing at the same time.

"Whoo, that was brilliant I haven't run like that for, well, nearly three years. Amazing thanks again Max" he turned and smiled at her.

"You are very welcome" She smiled back.

"I am also enjoying being corporeal, or as near to it as I can get." She said. "It is quite liberating. Thank you for suggesting it."

"No worries." He gasped still recovering.

They got into the lift and made their way back to the transit room and from there back to the vault.

Paul and Izzy climbed the stairs and walked to meet Arawn. He pulled up moments after they arrived at the gate in the wall.

"Hi" Arawn said "How did you get on?"

"Long story I'll bring you up to date later" Paul said. He opened the back of the Land Rover which was stacked high with shopping.

"My God did you buy the whole supermarket?" Paul asked.

"Just the basics" Arawn replied. "Help me get it into the ship."

"I don't know if we can carry all of this. It'll take forever. I've got an idea" he said.

It was approaching four o'clock in the afternoon and darkness was closing in.

"Let's give it another hour or so until it's completely dark and we'll take the land rover into the field I saw about half a mile back. There are two transport shuttles on board the Maxsar that the Land Rover could easily drive into. Let's just drive it all onboard."

Paul got his mobile out and called Max. He explained his idea and asked if she could pilot one of the shuttles down to the field after dark.

They drove to the field which was quite secluded and parked in an out of the way spot. Paul fed Izzy and they shared the sandwiches and drinks Arawn had bought, and of course Izzy got a good share too. She insisted!

"So" Arawn said between mouths full. "What's been occurring?"

"Blimey where to start..." So Paul told him all that had transpired.

Arawn was amazed at the medical treatment Paul had received and made a note to himself to have a check up as well.

"A woman?" he interrupted Paul incredulously. "Well that will take some adjusting to." He laughed.

"I know but she's still the same Max only it's much easier to have someone to talk at if you see what I mean. And she is not bad to look at either. God listen to me? Letch of the year, Louise would kill me if she heard me saying this."

They both laughed.

It was now fully dark and Paul's phone vibrated. It was Max

"Hi" he answered.

"This is Max" She replied.

"Yes I know it is." He smiled rolling his eyes at Arawn who chuckled.

"The shuttle has just left the hangar and will be with you in five minutes and seventeen seconds" she said.

"Can you land with the ramp down ready?" Paul asked. "I don't want to risk the chance of some passers by seeing anything so the quicker we can get onboard the better." He said

"That will not be a problem" She replied.

"Ok we'll see you in a few minutes." Paul closed the connection

He looked at the phone and there in a small banner at the top of the screen was a timer. It currently was showing 3:45 and counting down.

Paul shook his head. "Brilliant" he said. Showing the phone to Arawn who smiled and nodded.

The countdown continued and bang on zero they saw two identical indentations appear in the field about fifty metres to their right. Suddenly appearing, visible in front of them was the lowering access ramp. Paul started up the land Rover, selected four wheel drive and drove towards the ramp as quickly as he dared. He didn't want to leave suspicious tyre tracks that appeared to drive into the field then stop. That would look odd to the farmer. He chuckled at the thought.

They reached the ramp and although it was fairly steep the Land rover coped superbly. They drove into the cargo bay, the ramp closing up behind them.

Arawn got out and looked around. "Nice." He said.

"I know" Paul replied. "Let's go up to the cockpit we should get a good view."

They climbed up and entered a fairly spacious cockpit with three bucket seats the centre one had flying controls and the other two sat in front of silent consoles.

Paul took the middle pilots seat and Arawn the one on the left. The shuttle was already lifting off. As they moved, straps appeared out of the seats automatically and secured them snugly.

Izzy had had to stay in the Land Rover as she hadn't really mastered the art of climbing ladders particularly well and she was safer in her 'hammock'.

Paul thought *"Izzy are you ok?"*

"Yes good" she replied.

He smiled. Arawn saw it and asked "What s funny?"

"Oh Nothing... I just talked to Izzy that's all" tapping his forehead "my dog!"

They both laughed and shook their heads. What a trip!

The almost vertical flight over Anglesey was a bit boring because it was too dark to see anything.

But once they broke through the cloud layer it was spectacular. Arawn gasped. Paul was used to night flying but it still was breathtaking.

The Maxsar wasn't visible to earth technology or even the number 1 eyeball. However, the windows on the shuttle also doubled as a heads up display and showed the Maxsar clearly. It steadily grew bigger by the minute. Paul hadn't seen her from the outside yet and he looked at every inch. The rear had three gigantic bell shaped engines each one was glowing a gentle blue. The Plasma cannon sat on the top on the port side towards the rear. A bulge like a semi submerged pipe ran from the rear all of the way to the front. It was open at the front Paul assumed it was the kinetic weapon or rail gun. There were other domes and turrets on the top side port and starboard and repeated underneath that he assumed were probably the point defence weapons.

The shuttle flew underneath and turned her nose towards Maxsar's flank where a dark, square hole was waiting. It reminded Paul of the event horizon in the vault. It was probably similar technology that allowed the passage of solid objects like a spaceship into the hangar but must keep the air inside. He thought

They passed through uneventfully and executed a perfect landing on the deck.

The straps released automatically and retracted into the seats. They got up and descended to the shuttles main deck. The rear ramp was opening already so they got into the Land Rover and drove out into the Hangar.

Paul parked with the back of the Land Rover towards the door he and Max had come through earlier ready to unload.

Max appeared outside. Paul and Arawn got out and Paul introduced Arawn to Max.

"It's nice having someone else to talk to" said Arawn making small talk. Paul could see Arawn was trying his best NOT to ogle Max.

He walked passed Arawn and pretending to trip up said "ooh sorry Arawn was that your tongue I just tripped over"

They both laughed. Arawn said "Yeah sorry Max. No offence. I will behave professionally from now on."

"That's ok" she said. "I don't really understand what's happening anyway" and smiled.

Arawn looked relieved.

Paul asked "is there any way we can get all of this stuff to the replicators in the cafeteria?" he asked.

"No problem" Max said and almost straight away two flat topped robots appeared out of hatches in the wall.

They loaded everything on to the robots and they drove off.

Two more robots appeared to take Paul and Arawns personal stuff to their private quarters.

They made their way back to the cafeteria where all of the food and drink needed to be scanned and catalogued into the replicators by hand which took a while.

Once that was done Paul suggested they have dinner and try and relax.

Paul perused the menus on the replicators.

"Now we're talking" he said. "Proper food excellent" He chose Steak and chips with a pepper sauce. The replicator even asked how he wanted it cooked. He hadn't catalogued the stakes.

"That was a good idea getting three different stakes"

"I got takeaways from various restaurants and provided three different types of stake, rare, medium and well done."

"How did you get restaurants to open up at that time of day?" asked Paul

"Erm… remember the piles of cash?"

"Oh yes" Paul laughed.

"We've got dishes from most types of cuisine. Chinese, Indian, Mexican, Italian, burgers, fried chicken. I bought virtually one of everything from every restaurant and takeaway that I could find open or at least with a chef present who didn't mind opening with a little incentive."

"Then I bought all sorts of things I figured we might need from the supermarket; toiletries, chocolate, beer, soft drinks, bread, bagels, crumpets, cookies and biscuits even cream cakes. So I apologise now if I've forgotten anything. There's even a really decent choice of wines? Although I don't suppose we should be drunk in charge of a spaceship" he laughed.

"Well we won't go hungry" Paul said.

They ate in silence. The food was excellent. Izzy enjoyed some steak and asked for *"more please"* Paul smiled. *"Sorry it'll bung you up"* He thought back.

"Doh!" thought Izzy

"Where did you pick up that word?" Paul thought

"You" she replied a strange thought came to him from her which he didn't immediately understand. Then it hit him.

"You're laughing!" He said

"Yes, is funny!" she replied.

He burst out laughing.

Arawn looked and asked calmly, as he was getting used to the silent conversations and was a little jealous too. "What now?" he said

"Izzy laughs!" said Paul

Arawn smiled and nodded "That's so cool" he said.

Arawn looked at Max who was sitting at the table with them.

"Max, is there any way I can enhance my telepathy gene? It's getting very lonely sitting here, with you all talking to each other."

"Yes. You will need a modified version of the serum, as you have partial enhancement already. We can proceed now if you like?"

"Yes please." He replied.

A short while later they were all in the medical bay. Arawn seeing it for the first time was blown away when Paul explained what Max had told him.

"Just think what we could do with this on Earth" he said.

"I know, but surely we need to find out what the situation is with the Tylvor first?"

"Yes agreed." he said.

Max instructed Arawn to lie on one of the medical couches. One of the arms retrieved a vial from a compartment in the side of itself and was injected into Arawn's neck.

He lay there staring into space.

"Arawn" Paul thought

Arawn jerked his head around and looked at Paul his eyes wide.

"OH MY WORD!" He shouted back.

Paul laughed *"I see what you meant earlier max, about newbie's shouting"*

"SORRY", *"Sorry"* he said repeating it and managing to turn the volume down.

"This is weird. Hi Izzy!" he thought

"Hi Arawn" Izzy replied in a different voice.

Paul had sounded like Paul and Izzy sounded like... well, presumably herself, because he'd never heard her speak before.

"Incredible" he said

"Yes is good" Izzy replied to him. He realised he was still talking to Izzy. He hadn't intentionally directed his thought at Izzy it was as if he'd left the connection to her open like a mobile phone call.

"Did you all hear the talk with Izzy?" he asked in his normal voice.

"No" said Paul "It's like a private phone call if you direct it at someone specific by thinking of them only. You can do what I think of as a wide broadcast and everyone will hear it. In a military scenario it would be very handy. Can you imagine if the SAS had that kind of power?"

"Can you all hear this?" He aimed at everyone.

"Yes" all three replied.

Arawn laughed and offered Paul a high five which he took turned to Max and offered the same. But she looked perplexed and didn't move.

"It's a sort of physical celebration of achievement or perhaps pleasure?" explained Paul "usually shared between team members when something has been successful"

"I see" She said "although, I cannot do it as you would physically pass through my hand"

Paul held his hand up anyway and she did likewise they tried to slap but as she said Pauls hand passed through hers. However, he did feel a tingle of some sort.

"I felt something there Max" He told her.

"Really? How interesting" she replied. "Perhaps there is something in that hmm..." She finished a look of deep thought on her face.

Paul said "Did you know you are developing human like facial expressions?"

Max looked at him and smiled "It is as a result of observations I have made of all of you." She replied.

"Oh really, and what did you pick up from Izzy?" Arawn laughed.

In less than a second Max's face morphed into what could only be described as a werewolf complete with the ears, the massive canines and the slavering jaw, she uttered the most terrifying growl at Arawn who jumped a mile and went white as a sheet.

Her face reverted to normal instantly and a satisfied smile replaced the previous look.

"One or two things?" she smiled.

"Bloody hell!" Arawn said.

Paul laughed and Izzy looked at Max in awe.

They made their way back to the private quarters and Arawn inspected his which was across the way from the captain's cabin. As he walked towards the door he saw the sign said Executive officer.

"What's an executive officer?" he asked

"Usually they are the second in command" said Paul. "It's your position if you want it? I am temporary Captain, until we find a Madden to replace me. So we need someone who can do other things for the moment."

"Ok why not. It's only for a few weeks right?"

"Yep, should be"

He stepped up to the door and walked into his quarters. "They were laid out almost identically to Pauls. He inspected the facilities and thoroughly approved.

"Nice" he said. "I've never had anywhere as nice as this before. I've only got a bedsit"

"Well its late, I think we should get some kip and tomorrow we can make a start?"

"Why tomorrow, captain?" Max asked.

"I have no idea" he replied. Realising that with Max flying the ship there was no need to wait.

"Ok Max. How long is the trip to the nearest Madden outpost?"

"Approximately 12 hours." She replied.

"Ok let's get going. Can you wake us up in say 8 hours time please?"

"Yes of course." She replied. They all felt a deep base rumble in the ship as the engines fired up. It faded after a few seconds, after they had overcome the ships inertia and managed to get her moving through space.

"Excellent. Well, good night to you both" Paul said and with Izzy following he left them in Arawn's suite.

Arawn asked. "Can I operate all of the devices by telepathy now Max?"

"Indeed. Think what you want to do and try to direct it, as you directed your thoughts to Izzy earlier, to the device you wish"

"Ok" he said. *"Display on"* he thought directing at the curved screen on the wall above the console.

As in the captains quarters it activated duplicating the bridge display. What he saw was astounding. A visual of the solar system, but all of the planets were moving away at great speed.

"Where are we heading?" he asked.

"To one of the Sol passage points it is located about forty five degrees above the plane of the ecliptic in line with the Kuiper belt. In fact the fragments of rock and ice that make up the Kuiper belt also help to hide the passage point. We should arrive there within twenty minutes."

"Does Paul know?"

"No, I will inform him" She transmitted her thoughts to Paul who replied that he would like to be on the bridge when they transited the passage point.

"He would like to see the passage point transit on the bridge."

"Yes me too" said Arawn "I just need to use the facilities" he said and walked into the bathroom.

Max followed him and stood watching. "Erm, on my own please?" he said.

"Oh I am sorry is this typical human behaviour?" she asked.

"Yes people like their privacy when going to the toilet, bathing, dressing etc."

"Indeed. I will deactivate for now." And she vanished.

"Right... see you in a bit" Arawn said to no one in particular.

Ten minutes later they were all on the bridge.

Paul took the main command chair and suggested to Arawn he take one of the other consoles.

He chose the left hand one and activated the console. It illuminated and Paul suggested he familiarise himself with the weapons system first. Arawn busied himself scrolling through screens.

Paul changed the main display to show countdown to their destination and a chart of the surrounding area.

They could see a misty band of particles that was the Kuiper belt. It consisted mostly of ice with some rocks mixed in as well. Pluto was a considerable distance off to one side and was indicated with a tag and a larger icon.

On the screen dead ahead was a gradually increasing icon with the tag PP against it. Paul focused on the PP and thought *"More Info"* the tag expanded into text showing technical information he didn't really understand but some data did make sense. Distance to the PP, power showed as 5.6Yw.

"Max what does Yw mean? Next to the power reading on the screen"

"Yotawatts in Earth scale"

"What's the difference between a Terawatt and a Yotawatt? I'm sure I've read somewhere for example that earth produces about twenty eight thousand Terawatts per hour of electrical power. What's the output of the power generator?"

"Earth produces 2.8×10^{14} Tw. The power generator produces 5.6×10^{24} Yw." she replied.

Paul and Arawn both gasped at the power generated.

He looked at the dimensions of the power generator. It was a sphere about one kilometre in diameter, unbelievable.

"How do the passage points work?"

"The exact mechanisms of the passage points are not known to me. They were developed hundreds of thousands of years ago and I am not required to understand the extremely complex mathematics and the science behind them. I do know they are opened by an emission of neutrons in a coded burst; each code is particular to each passage point. It can be projected onto the area in space where the passage will open or onto the generator itself. An energy envelope is generated around the ship and we accelerate into the opening to be sent to the destination point. The energy envelope sustains our transit. We exit at the other end of the passage point at the same velocity we entered. So it is advisable to be cautious."

"What if we meet another ship coming the other way?" Arawn asked.

"It is not possible. The mathematics dictates that simultaneous transit in both directions is permissible."

"And what if another ship is trying to dive into the opening at the other end at the moment we pop out?" Said Paul

"The power generators at both ends are equipped with scanners and part of their function is to allow a secure exit. In the event of a possible collision it will automatically divert the exit point to another location within ten thousand kilometres in any direction thus preventing accidents."

"That's good to know" smiled Paul. "Are there any relativistic effects?"

"Any what now?" asked Arawn laughing

"You know, you've read sci-fi books haven't you?" If we travel near the speed of light things slow down for us. But continue at the same speed for those left behind."

"Ah yes heard something about that..." he grinned. "Guess I'll have to do some reading then!"

"No there are no relativistic effects as you currently understand it. Time at both the entry point and exit point continues at the same rate as that on board the ship in transit.

So an hour on board is an hour at the departure point and at the arrival point" Max explained.

"Excellent. No time travel then?" Paul laughed.

"No." Max said as if talking to an errant schoolboy.

"5 minutes." Said Arawn

Paul returned his attention to the screen. The passage point appeared much bigger now and was showing more information. A series of numbers and letters transited across the screen below it too quickly for Paul to catch.

"What was that Max?"

"That is a query sent by the generator. I have replied with the correct code. It should give us the coordinates to the entry point next."

"So like IFF?" he asked.

"IFF?" she queried.

"Yes on fighter planes we have an Identification Friend or Foe system which operates in a similar way. A signal is sent from one aircraft and a reply is returned with the correct codes to identify a friend or if not they must be an enemy."

"In principle it is similar. Only this involves several hundred thousand bytes of information."

"Of course it does." Said Paul smiling, "always one better" he muttered quietly.

"I didn't hear your last sentence." Max said.

"That's ok it wasn't important. Are they the coordinates?" he asked as more data flashed across the screen below the passage point icon.

"Yes altering course now." Max replied

The whole screen began to turn to the left. A reticule appeared on the main screen in green and a green dot off to the left moved towards the centre of the reticule a distance readout and descending course angle appeared in the reticule.

The ship gradually brought the dot into the centre of the reticule where it remained.

Max said "Firing the neutron burst now." A symbol appeared in the reticule around the green dot that represented the area they were aiming for.

A luminous cloudy whirlpool began to form with a dark centre began expanding reached a certain diameter and stopped. A shimmering blue light covered the whole of the screen as the ship continued to travel forwards towards the dark opening.

Paul felt himself tense up and he gripped the arms of the command chair so tightly his knuckles turned white.

They entered the passage point and for a couple of milliseconds he got a feeling of stretching off into the distance. It passed almost instantly but left a slight feeling of nausea. He had never been air sick even when pulling 5 or 6 gees in a tight turn in his F35.

He glanced at Arawn. Oh dear, he had gone as white as a sheet.

"Max do we have sick bags?" he asked quietly while pointing at Arawn

She looked over and said "Ah yes I think there are suitable receptacles in the console in front. Think drawer" she smiled.

Paul thought *"drawer"* and directed it at Arawn's console. Sure enough a drawer opened and there were various items, some of which were sick bag like.

"Arawn" he said

Arawn turned.

"In the drawer if required." He said pointing then miming holding one up to his mouth.

"Ah, yes thanks. I think I'm ok but nice to know they're there." He smiled weakly.

The main screen had now changed to an overall darkness with the occasional streak of feint light shooting past them. Not as interesting as some of the sci-fi shows he'd watched.

"Is there anything we need to do duties wise Max?" he asked.

"Normally, yes, the bridge is permanently manned but I can manage everything for now. If you wish to retire I will wake you one hour before we arrive"

"That's great. Don't know about you Arawn but I'm off for a shower and bed."

"Yeah me too I'm whacked. What a day!" he replied.

"Max, I haven't given it a thought but where can Izzy do her, you know her business."

"Do you mean, urinate and defecate?"

"Yes!" he chuckled

At the end of the quarters corridor there is a, what you would call a park?"

"A park, on a spaceship, really..."

"Yes" she said with a note of finality.

"Ok...Yes, what a day indeed. Come on Izz" he said walking out

Paul and Izzy walked off the bridge and past the captain's quarters down to the end of the corridor.

Arawn retired to the XO's rooms.

At the end of the corridor there was a door with, sure enough a label that simply said Recreation area. He walked up to it and as per usual it opened with a swish.

There in front of him was a park. He gazed in slack jawed amazement. The room was as big as the hangars were. There was a dome over the top with artificial lighting that hinted at a sun that had just set. There were trees, actual trees and grass and flowers. There was even a stream running through the grounds. Benches were placed at various locations gazebos, and other structures were dotted about. It must have been a hundred and fifty metres by two hundred metres by at least fifty or sixty metres high. There was even a slight rise he could see in amongst the trees in front of him..

"Ball!" shouted Izzy... who bounded away sniffing at everything.

Paul laughed. He looked around the perimeter. He could see furniture and what looked like stalls with benches and tables close by set near the walls. He walked over and realised they were eating places possibly cafes? The Madden would have used this place for relaxing with friends. A feeling of sadness came over him as he remembered the Madden crew had all been killed. It would have been nice to watch and listen to this place when it was busy.

He started to walk along one of the paths under the trees. The first trees he looked at were very familiar closely resembling Oak he moved on and saw Mountain Ash, Silver Birch there were even some mature Cedars.

Flowers bloomed scattered randomly underneath the trees or in formal beds.

The ship never ceased to amaze him. He looked for Izzy who had just completed phase two of her 'business' which he felt he should tidy up. Searching his pockets the only thing he had was some kitchen towel he usually carried as a handkerchief. "That'll do" he thought. He walked over to the spot in question or at least he thought that was where Izzy had done it! But there was nothing there.

"Max?" he thought

"Yes?"

"I am in the park, which is mind blowing by the way, and Izzy has just finished her toilet, but I can't find it to clear it up! I have lost a poo!"

"There is no requirement to clear up. The pico nanites manage that sort of thing. They convert it into fertilizer for the gardens"

"Ok thanks, as I said earlier... What a day!" and he smiled.

"Come on Izz time for bed" He said.

"No ball?" She asked cocking her head to the side and looking at him.

"Just too tired," he said. *"Tomorrow definitely"*

"OK" she replied.

On returning to his cabin Paul discovered there was a small replicator in the main living area he hadn't noticed before and he ordered up a couple of towels, some shower gel and a razor. He undressed and ran the shower. It was luxurious. He stood under the powerful jets of hot water and let it massage his neck and shoulders.

He hadn't been pain free for a long time and it was fantastic.

He turned off the shower, stepped out and towelled himself dry, stood in front of the sink and proceeded to shave off the few days of beard.

Feeling so much better he walked into the bedroom, pulled back the covers sat down and was just about to lie down when he remembered *'ball'*

He smiled, walked over to the replicator and managed to locate in the Madden dog section, a rubber ball of all things. He took it out test bounced it a couple of times and threw it to Izzy who caught it in mid air she thought it was brilliant. She jumped up on the bed and settled down with her new toy.

Finally, he got into bed, laid down managed to pull the covers over himself before he fell into a deep sleep the like of which he hadn't had in a long time.

Chapter 7

Paul yawned and stretched in bed. He couldn't remember having a better night's sleep in years.

"Good morning Max. How are we doing?" he asked

"Good morning captain. We are 1.5 hours out from our destination." Her voice came out of hidden speakers somewhere in the room.

"OK. Can you give Arawn a wakeup call please?"

"He got up earlier and has been taking a tour of the ship." She replied.

"That's good." He said pleased Arawn was using his initiative. "I'll meet you on the bridge in a while."

"Yes captain"

"Max, the uniform you appear to wear, is it more than just clothing? "

"Yes Captain, the version for live beings is an environmental suit that protects the user from radiation; it has built in communications, and an automatic head covering in the event of decompression. It can supply breathable air for up to 4 hours. It can even protect the wearer in the vacuum of space for up to ten minutes. Also it has magnetic boots for use during zero or greatly reduced gravity"

"Can we replicate one each for me and Arawn? Do you wear undergarments with them or do they self clean?"

"They are self cleaning."

"Cool. Where can we pick them up?"

"A service robot will deliver them in the next ten minutes."

"Thanks. Come on Izz lets go for a walk" he called.

She came trotting out of the bedroom. He picked up the ball and they walked down the corridor into the park.

Back in his quarters a while later, he fed Izzy and sat on one of the arm chairs and enjoyed his coffee from the replicator. It was actually quite good coffee.

There was a suit waiting on the bed and matching boots on the floor.

Next to it he found a smaller pile of the material with six gaps which were presumably for appendages.

"Max?" Just checking, but what's this other suit for?

"Izzy" she replied.

"Brilliant!" he laughed.

He donned his own and put the boots on without socks. They really were comfortable. They were thin and yet he could feel they were tough at the same time. He stood up walked over to the view screen and thought *"Screen, mirror"*. It changed to a mirror finish allowing him to inspect himself. The suit looked good, but he didn't. The suit was bulging a little too much, in places.

"Have to cut down on the old steak and chips eh Izz?"

"Steak!" came back. Paul laughed.

His badge said Capt. Arwyn and on his shoulder he had four thin rank bars embedded into the material but slightly lighter in colour, similar to the old Wing Commander bars he had in the RAF.

He called Izzy over and she sniffed at her suit suspiciously

"What is it?" she thought

"It's the same as I am wearing but for you"

"Ok" she thought.

Paul managed to get her in to it with a little difficulty. All appendages and spaces for vital activities were in the right place. Someone had put in a great deal of thought to doggy functions. The feet seemed to be hardened like his boots. It covered her tail, but exposed her rear areas! (That's how Paul thought of them and chuckled) oh and her head of course.

Izzy was as good as gold she didn't struggle and let Paul fit the suit. It took a bit of experimentation to find the easiest way to do it.

Once it was on he stood up and looked at her. He smiled she looked really cool. It even had a name plate like his but one on each shoulder.

"Max, will Izzy's suit seal up over all the right areas in an emergency?" he asked aloud.

"Indeed. She can wear it constantly. As yours does, it allows the body and skin to breath. It is self cleaning and it maintains a constant skin temperature even down to absolute zero, but, as with yours in those conditions, only for ten minutes."

"Excellent." he said "I notice there are pads or thicker areas of material on the back and hips. What are they for?"

"The pads on the back are where the energy generators are kept. But the hip areas are for attaching weapons or other items."

"Ah, right. Talking of weapons should we be armed?"

"I would certainly recommend it when we arrive at the destination" She said.

"Is there an armoury on board?"

"Yes. If you wish to avail yourself we should go now as we do not have much time before we arrive."

"Arawn" Paul thought

"Hi, what's up?" a reply came back. Again, Paul thought, how cool telepathy is.

"We're going to the armoury before we arrive at the Madden outpost. Can you meet us there in five?" Paul asked.

"Aye Aye captain!" he said

Paul didn't reply, still a little uncomfortable with the title, although he should be used to it after his years in the RAF. As usual Max provided arrows to the armoury which was on the same level as the bridge but towards the rear of the ship.

Arawn and Max were waiting inside when Paul and Izzy arrived.

Arawn had his suit on. Paul noticed he had a two bar rank on his shoulders and his badge said Lt. Griffiths.

"Morning" Arawn said. "I've had a great tour. How amazing is the park. Have you seen the waterfall?" he asked.

"Cool outfit Izz!" He thought to everyone.

"Cool!" she replied and gave a vocal yip, which made them both chuckle.

"No, I haven't seen the waterfall yet!" Paul exclaimed smiling.

He looked around the room. There were racks of different weapons. There were pistols, what he thought of as rifles, some really big rifles much thicker and heavier and some small trays of items that could well be grenades of some sort with three different colours.

"Is there a practice range we could use Max?"

"Yes through the door on your left.

Paul selected one of the smaller pistol type weapons and touched it to his hip where it adhered to one of the thicker areas.

He picked up a couple of the grenades and stuck them on the opposite hip. He hefted a normal rifle and one of the much bigger ones. He was surprised how light they were. He had always associated power and destructive capacity with mass and wondered if these were as good as they looked.

A section he had missed initially contained knives. They were about the size of what he knew as a Bowie knife and came complete with a sheath.

He selected one and looking at his hips, which were now full, he asked Max. "Where can I keep this knife?"

"The sheath will adhere to any part of your uniform. You do not necessarily need to attach them all to your hip. Be extremely careful. The blade is honed down to a single molecule it can cut through almost any material with extreme ease."

So he stuck it on the side of his leg. It held.

Arawn helped himself to a selection as well. They looked like a couple of mercenaries from a film as they entered the practice range.

They found a row of booths similar to firing ranges back at home. Paul set up in one with Arawn immediately next door to him. Max took station behind and between them.

"How do these work then Max? Are they projectile weapons?"

"The small pistol is a simple but powerful laser. The medium sized rifle fires metal projectiles electrically accelerated a hand held rail gun. The largest is a plasma rifle. They are all coded to your DNA. And operate by thought. Think *"On"* or *"Off"*, then simply aim and pull the trigger with your finger. For safety and in combat situations, if you let go of them they immediately turn off."

Paul picked up the pistol thought *"On"* he felt a gentle hum in his hand. He aimed at a target and squeezed. There was no recoil at all. A small hole appeared on the target with a small curl of smoke.

"I can't see anything he said. I expected, I don't know, bolts of light flying towards the target" he chuckled.

"Why?" Max asked. "It is a light energy weapon, light is not visible unless it reflects off something."

Ok he thought let's have a go with the gauss rifle. He picked it up and turned it on, aimed and fired. There was a small amount of recoil which made it feel like a weapon Paul was used to firing. A larger hole appeared in the target this time. Much more satisfying he thought.

"And now on to the big beastie" he said, hefting the plasma rifle. He aimed at the target, activated the rifle and fired. There was a millisecond delay before an oval pulse of super heated plasma erupted from the front of the weapon, it travelled fast towards the target and when it hit, it didn't just punch a hole, it clung to the target, melting or burning it completely.

"Wow, that's scary" he said.

Arawn had been watching and he now turned eagerly to have a go himself.

He tried all of the weapons in turn. Then he pulled out one of the grenades.

"Be careful with the red ones" said Max. "They are plasma grenades, you have seen what the rifles can do, these, scatter plasma in all directions and have a range of about ten metres." she added.

"Ok... being careful" said Arawn. He picked up a red Plasma grenade thought *"On"* a small round area illuminated.

"Touch the area, and then throw it. There is a delay after throwing. The default is ten seconds but can be reduced or increased if you think It." said Max.

Arawn pressed it and threw it into the range. A visible shimmering shield instantly appeared between them and the grenade.

The grenade exploded in an intensely bright, expanding ball of plasma and rushed out to a diameter of about 10 metres as Max had said. It engulfed various target items that were arrayed in the range and within a few seconds they had melted entirely.

"What did I do?" asked Arawn pointing at the shimmer in front of them.

"Nothing, there is an automated shield that detects the weapon types being used and activates automatically for your protection" Max replied.

"That's good!" He said.

Paul picked up a blue grenade. Primed it, this time thought *"Timer 5 seconds"* and threw it. The automatic shield appeared again. The grenade exploded like Paul expected. Similar to Earth type shock grenades or flash bangs as he knew them. They were designed to stun or temporarily disorientate people.

Paul asked. "Max how impervious to weapons is the suit?"

"Not at all" She replied. "All of the weapons would penetrate or destroy the suits. However, we do have armoured suits. These are designed for battle. They are extremely complex. We do not have time now to go into details. But they are available for use when needed."

"Ok" Said Paul. "Let's head back to the bridge. I think we've got a lot to do."

Paul sat in the command chair, Arawn the weapons position. The screen was still showing the passage point, the blankness of which only disturbed by an occasional streak of light that came towards the ship and flew past incredibly quickly.

The countdown timer showed 30 seconds. Paul tensed in anticipation. On zero the screen refreshed and returned to normal, though the view was very different. There were far fewer stars visible. He thought *"show a slow sweep 360 degrees same plane"* The screen began to move showing the view around the ship. As it swept round the Milky Way came into view and then rotated out of sight back to the original position.

A green dot on the screen and a tag identified it as "Coloon base" It orbited a rocky barren planet with a label of XG876. There was a white dwarf star at the centre of the system and at least eight other bodies that classed as planets and one gas giant. There were no habitable planets.

Paul thought *"all stop"* and the ship slowed to a halt.

"Max, are we completely invisible?" he asked

"Yes we are fully cloaked" she replied.

"Can we scan the area without revealing ourselves?"

"Yes, using passive scans but it will take longer than using active scans"

"Well were not in a hurry. Let's do that please. How long will it take?"

"About five minutes" She replied.

"Out of interest, how long would an active scan take?" he asked for future reference.

"30 seconds" she replied.

"Ok, noted."

A countdown had appeared on screen and Paul watched it eagerly. The scan results showed there was almost nothing else out here apart from some scattered interstellar dust, the occasional asteroid and the Coloon base. As for the base itself it didn't register any life signs, or in fact any heat or any other radiation of any sort except for a faint intermittent signal coming from somewhere inside.

He opened the tag and read the details on Coloon. It was a space station approximately 12 by 12 by 3 kilometres in size. Its surface was covered in tall aerials, dishes, and other projections and nodules. Overall it was a square shape with rounded edges. It carried a crew of 2500. It could service three Madden warships at any time, and was a relay station for FTL communications.

That last bit of information interested Paul.

"Max what is FTL communications, what are its capabilities and are we equipped with it?"

"Unfortunately we are not. The station has it, but it is large, and would place too great a burden on our power capacity. Also you must be stationary to use it. It can however, provide instant communications over tens of thousands of light years. You can communicate instantly from almost one side of the galaxy to the other at its narrowest point. Messages sent along the longest axis of the galaxy would take approximately two hours to be sent and a reply received."

"That is incredibly impressive. Could we use it to contact anyone, because I'm not optimistic here? In fact it looks like this station is lifeless."

"That is possible and I agree the station looks as if it has been abandoned for a long time."

"The intermittent signal we are picking up can you tell what it is?"

"It is a Madden locator beacon, but extremely weak. Perhaps we should investigate?"

"Yes I don't see why not. It will be a good familiarisation and acclimatisation exercise for our equipment."

"Can we dock anywhere?"

"Yes there is a docking bay in the centre of the screen as we are looking at it."

"Thanks. I think I need to do this myself but could you oversee it please in case I need assistance?"

"Yes captain" she replied.

Paul took control. He increased the ship speed to a crawl as they approached when they reached 10 kilometres out, a reticule appeared and identified a matching location on the station at about 5 o'clock on the screen. He guided the reticule onto the destination target and continued slowing almost to a standstill. A velocity indicator had popped up and showed in green. At one point he increased their speed but the indicator turned red.

"Ok not that fast" he muttered and backed off until it turned green again. The point at which the velocity indicator turned red began to creep down, in effect guiding Paul at the correct speed until they arrived at the docking point and barely kissed the station. It was easier than Paul had thought. It *was* easier than landing an F35 on an aircraft carrier especially in rough seas.

A gentle clunk was felt rather than heard through the ship.

Green indicators popped up on the screen showing a good dock.

"Well done captain" said Max. "You appear to be a natural"

"Yes good job" agreed Arawn.

"Is there atmosphere on board? Or do we need to use our suits?"

"As far as I can ascertain the atmosphere is good which would indicate no decompression. "

Arawn asked "Could it have been decompressed but maintenance bots fixed it afterwards?"

"Yes that is a possibility. We will find out shortly."

"Captain, can you carry an extra item with you please?"

"Sure yes what do you want me to take?"

She turned as a hatch opened and a bot rolled out with a small silver cube about 5cms square. It stopped by Paul. He bent down and picked it up.

"What is it?" he asked.

"It is a portable holographic projector. It will allow me to accompany you outside of the ship."

"That's great. Will it be ok if Izzy carried it?"

"Of course" she smiled.

"No problem. Let's go then. Max, lead the way please." He touched the cube to Izzy's back and it stayed in position.

"Look after that Izzy. It's Max" he thought to her.

"Max. Like Max" she replied. Paul smiled, good, we're bonding.

They exited the bridge and took an elevator which travelled forwards and down. It opened into a larger than normal corridor with a large heavy door at one end with a transparent window in it. A red panel was illuminated to one side

Paul looked through when they arrived and realised it must be an airlock of some sort.

"Press the panel Captain" Max asked.

He did so, they heard a faint hiss and after a delay of a few seconds the panel turned green and the door hinged open inwards. The door was at least 5m high and 5 wide the airlock itself had the same dimensions and was at least 15m long.

"Max why is the airlock so large?" he asked

"So that larger pieces of equipment and supplies can be brought in if necessary and also armoured soldiers can mount a boarding party four a breast if required."

"Right, interesting" he said

The door automatically closed behind them and the panel on the door in front illuminated red. Paul pressed this one and the door opened into the station.

It was dark and cold but the air smelt ok it had feint whiff of age and dust perhaps? They were in a corridor with the same dimensions as the airlock. Presumably all a standard design Paul thought.

There were the same large doors either side of them and a smaller door where they were heading.

"Think to your suit and activate your visors" Max said.

"Visor" Both Paul and Arawn thought.

A head covering grew out of the collar of Paul's suit and brought a clear semi circular screen down over his eyes and level with the end of his nose. It illuminated with information.

"That's neat" he said. "Can you add directions to the signal we have seen please Max?"

"You can think it yourself captain. It would be better if you got used to doing it because I may not always be around"

"True" he said. "Ok here goes"

How should I phrase this? *"Show direction to locator beacon"* Instantly a flashing dot appeared in the top left hand corner of the visor with an arrow next to it pointing forwards and a readout of distance in metres. It wasn't obtrusive and Paul could still see everything around him.

He found that the hood of the suit had also amplified the environmental sounds. He could hear Izzy panting, and Arawn's stomach grumbling.

He looked at Arawn who was looking at him they both smiled and nodded in appreciation.

They walked to the door which opened automatically. "How does this space station know we are friendly Max?"

"Via the suits they communicate automatically with all Madden tech"

"Good." He said.

They walked into the next corridor the tracker telling Paul to go left. They continued to walk for some ten minutes when the tracker indicated they turn left again through another slightly larger door. It indicated the beacon was 200 metres away.

The sign against this door said Hangar Four in Madden but Pauls visor provided a translation next to the word.

"Ok, before we enter, let's be careful. Weapons ready." He took out his pistol and turned it on. "Oh and let's communicate only by thought rather than give ourselves away if there's anything dangerous here."

"*Ok.*" thought Arawn.

He hadn't had much combat training, apart from the compulsory Aircrew SERE, Survive Evade Resist Extract training at RAF St Mawgan in Cornwall so was basically familiar with combat situations and he could competently handle firearms.

"*Izzy, stay close by me*"

"*Ok*" she replied.

The door opened silently and they stepped through into a hangar. It was bigger than those on the Maxsar, but there was only one ship. It was much smaller than the Maxsar about 400 metres in length by 150 metres wide by about 50 metres tall. About half way along its length there was a simple mobile stairway pushed up against a closed hatch much like an earth airliner. This ship looked really old and battered. If this had been an Earth ship Paul thought it would have duct tape all over it! There were even some items hanging off the body held on only by cables.

"*It is a Madden fast patrol ship*" thought Max to everyone.

"*Is it serviceable?*" Asked Paul

"I am not sure. It is possible, but if it is completely shutdown I cannot tell. Now we are this close I think the locator beacon is inside."

"Can anyone see us do you think?" Asked Paul

"I cannot sense any active scanners although passive infra red scanners would detect the heat from your exposed body parts" she added.

"Ok let's be alert" He said and walked forwards towards the steps. He reached the bottom, looked around and stepped on the first rung. He paused as if expecting something to happen. Nothing did so he continued making his way slowly up to the hatch.

At the top a panel illuminated in red. He pressed it, a few seconds passed and with a slight hiss the panel turned green and the hatch swung inwards and aside.

Paul stepped in Izzy at his side. She was sniffing the air furiously. Paul Looked at her and thought .

"What can you smell Izz?"

"People" she said.

"Did you all hear that?" Paul asked. "Yes" confirmed Arawn and Max.

"So extra careful, there is someone here."

They walked on *"Route to bridge"* he thought and the same directional arrow and distance appeared on the visor. It was only 50 metres. They walked slowly down the corridor, and came to the bridge door. It was as well built as the bridge door on the Maxsar but not as big. It opened automatically.

"So not everything is shut down?" Paul said.

"So it would appear." said *Max*.

They entered the bridge. Everything was off. This bridge was smaller than the Maxsar's with the usual command chair and only one other console. Paul walked to the command chair and sat down. Immediately everything came to life, the main view screen, the console in front of him and the command chair. He thought

"Internal scans life signs 3d" A holographic line drawing of the ship appeared in the space between the console and the command chair. It showed three green dots in the centre of the ship each with a label. It was them.

But that wasn't what drew Paul's attention. Showing two decks below them were three red dots...

While they were pondering their next move, a stealthed communications array sent a data burst from the Coloon station out towards a stealthed buoy near the other passage point.

Chapter 8

"Well, well, there are uninvited guests on board" Paul said. "Do you have any idea how they could take control of the ship Max?"

"Unfortunately, no, this is a worrying development if anyone can control a Madden ship." She replied.

Paul thought for a moment.

"We don't know if they're hostile or not. Max what can you find out from the ships logs?"

"Checking now captain" She paused. "Interesting, it would seem that one of them has the genetic mutation to access Madden tech. That would explain how they are on board. They are from a race called the Altarr. I am familiar with their language and history it would also appear that they have flown this vessel for over two years. They have travelled in many short journeys, with long periods when they are shutdown and cruising on minimal energy. They have used sixteen Passage points during that time. They originated much closer to the centre of the galaxy, from what is labelled as the Tylvor Empire." She sounded worried.

"Ok let's call them up telepathically and see how that goes. Does the system know their names?" Paul said.

"No other than 1, 2 and 3. Presumably they have been trying to keep, off the radar? I think you say?" replied Max.

"Probably" said Paul "Max, if I think to you, can you communicate with them please and provide a simultaneous translation?"

"Yes captain. Please begin" She said.

"My name is Paul. I am a human from the planet Earth, and we mean you no harm."

He waited, for what seemed like a minute before a reply came back.

From Max he received

"I am Martol and we do not wish to be enslaved. We will die first"

"Enslaved?" said Paul outraged. *"We are not slavers"* He thought, *"and we are not Tylvor"*

"Who you are then and why should we trust you?"

Paul thought how much should he tell them? But then again, trust was based on truth and openness and he had a feeling… So he told them most of what had transpired over the last few days. About finding the orb, Maxsar, the truth of what was happening out in the Galaxy.

There was a pause. Then

"We will meet you in the cafeteria." Said Martol

"Ok" Paul replied.

"Let's go guys." He said putting his weapon back on his hip.

The walk to the cafeteria was short and they arrived first. Paul sat them all down facing the door. Izzy at his feet.

About five minutes later the door opened and three very different aliens walked slowly through. The Altarr were tall, about six feet, two arms and two legs, with grey skin and a long face. They had holes where nostrils were on humans and small eyes. No ears that Paul could see. They were wearing grey robes and sandals exposing their three toed feet. They had matching thin hands with two fingers and opposable thumbs.

Paul stood and they immediately stopped. The front one looked at Paul's weapon on his hip. He glanced down at it, reached over with his opposite hand and detached it he leaned over and placed it slowly on the table out of his immediate reach. He looked at Arawn, who did the same.

"Visor" He thought and his visor and hood retracted back into the collar of his suit.

Arawn did likewise. Max had no need to as she didn't require the visor.

This seemed to settle the Altarr. They walked up to the table and bowed deeply.

Paul thought. *"I am Paul, This is Arawn and this is Max."* indicating each person in turn. A whine came from under the table. *"Oh and this is Izzy"* He indicated beneath them.

The Altarr stepped back looked under the table and collectively gasped. They immediately began talking in agitated voices to each other. The sound was slightly melodic, almost musical.

"What is the problem?" Paul thought, Max translating telepathically at the same time for all of them.

The lead Altarr spoke in his melodic way.

"I am Martol. This is Mannea my partner and this is our son Montar. Who are you really?

Paul was surprised at the question.

"I am sorry I don't understand?" he said.

"You have come to use from legend." Martol said.

Paul was completely confused.

"I think you've got us mixed up with someone else. I've come from Anglesey" he smiled.

"No! Do not insult us." said Martol vehemently. *"The prophecy is clear...two aliens, one Madden and a dog"*

"Please sit down, all of you, I think you had better tell us some more." Paul thought.

"Very well." Martol and the others sat themselves at the table and began to narrate a tale long in the making.

"Our story begins a long time ago my forefathers were happy. Our home planet Altarr was beautiful, rich in animal and plant life. We lived in peace. We traded ethically, we revered nature. Our scientists were clever. We achieved Space flight about 4000 years ago. This brought us to the attention of the Tylvor." He bent his head sadly and paused.

"They sent ships. At first only two appeared and observed us from orbit for several days. We realised they had travelled through a portal on the outskirts of our system. We tried to communicate with the. But they refused. We were concerned but not overly worried. These two ships departed. We had managed to station a primitive ship close by and they observed the method of their departure. Our scientists raced to develop the neutron beam that caused the portal to open. We were successful, and over the next few months they built a larger faster ship."

"They successfully opened the portal. After much debate they decided to send an envoy of three of our highest ranking ambassadors and a crew of fifteen. They travelled to the portal, opened it and proceeded through. We heard nothing for two months. Then one day, the portal opened and fifteen massive ships arrived. They destroyed the ship we had stationed there to monitor the portal with very little effort and proceeded to Altarr."

"What happened next was horrific and although it was four thousand years ago it still causes pain and despair in our hearts."

"The Tylvor as we now knew them to be for we did not know who they were in the beginning. They landed on our planet and using mechanised suits of armour, terrifying vehicles, weapons *of mass destruction and air ships, they systematically destroyed and enslaved our planet and people. They took millions away with them in huge transport ships."*

"My distant relatives hid along with a few hundred other refugees. They were terrified."

"For a period of several years no more was seen of these invaders. Until one day, a new ship arrived. They came in peace, or so they claimed, calling themselves the Tylvor. They said they were our allies and we should form a trading partnership. They would organise a government, help to rebuild. Our people were happy to accept all that they said.

A local government was created loyal and subservient to our saviours. The Tylvor are very good at propaganda, they made many of our people believe this was the best way forwards. They could offer access to other planets for trade. And all they wanted in return was food stuff, meat, grains, vegetables and fruits."

"They took nearly everything and left us to starve. They stationed soldiers on our planet who policed the harvests, arrested and eradicated people who objected. Soon what remained of our people were in abject poverty living only to fulfil the requirements of the Tylvor. They no longer needed any ships, as our people were completely broken and subjugated. The garrison of soldiers had enough ground and air vehicles to police the harvesting, and a freighter would arrive once a month to remove the proceeds."

"Time moved on and many years later the survivors that had escaped the initial attack were living in a secluded valley, being

extremely cautious and avoiding contact with anyone else they had eked out a living for a couple of hundred Altarrians and at the same time, kept it hidden from the Tylvor."

"A young male Altarrian who had decided to do some exploring away from the confines of the valley noticed a ship travelling low to the ground and heading for the valley. He ran as quickly as he could to sound the alarm."

"The ship landed quietly, and an alien the like of which we had not seen before appeared. At first we wondered if he was of the race that had invaded before the Tylvor arrived and proclaimed they were our saviours. He introduced himself as a Madden. He explained that he could take all of us away to live in peace and freedom on another planet if we wished."

"There were many people that said yes. But there was also a number who felt they had been fooled by one alien race before what made the Madden different?"

"Some stayed behind but my ancestors chose to go with the Madden. They escaped."

"A colony of Altarrians was set up on a pleasant planet. It was not Altarr by any means. But we thrived. The Madden were true to their word and helped us any way they could with technology, they even gave us some older ships that they had retired. Hence the ship you can see in the hangar. We had food, shelter, technology, access to space travel things were getting better. Many hundreds of years passed, some of us had accessed the gene technology of the Madden and developed telepathic abilities. An unforeseen side effect of this, was precognition. A tiny number of Altarrians probably no more than ten over a period of a hundred years or so became seers.

They could predict rainfall, crop failures and diseases. It was miraculous they became revered among our people. A seer called Algar who was destined to be the greatest seer and the last made a prophecy she foresaw the destruction of New Altarr and the coming of "Hope."

Martol paused. They all took a breath and Paul sat up straight.

After a few seconds he said "Please continue."

"Algar urged as many as would listen to leave as soon as possible before the Tylvor arrived. Many were sceptical. But those that could, left in the ships the Madden had given them and only just in time. For the Tylvor scout ships arrived in the system as they had done before. Only this time it wasn't months before they returned it was days. The same destruction and enslavement continued as previously."

"Algar and her followers had managed to escape. They continued travelling for as long as possible as far away from Tylvor space as possible."

"We finally settled another uninhabited planet and began to establish a community. Algar grew old but she refined, adjusted and recorded her prophecy. She stated that it would be many hundreds of years before it would come to pass when the galaxy would rise up and free from the terror of the Tylvor."

"And what did the prophecy say exactly?" Asked Paul.

"Hope will arrive carrying four companions. The magician. Two similar. One ancient and one different and young. The damaged one leads. The fair one counsels. The other and the *young one support. They will lead a vast armada. An unstoppable army and peace will reign for ten thousand years."*

"Well, four companions I suppose that matches, but as for the rest sorry, not us." said Paul not believing a word of it.

"As for a magician, that definitely rules us out, unless you count card tricks?" he added a little dismissively. He realised he'd been offensive.

"Sorry the last comment was not called for."

"We are not offended." said Martol.

"Hang on a sec" said Arawn. *"You* were badly injured or 'damaged' in many ways when we got together don't forget"

"Maxsar in Madden translates into English as 'Hope'." said Max quietly.

Paul was stunned. No, this can't be true its nonsense.

The young one what about that? That didn't match. But Izzy, she was only three years old.

The fair one counsels? Max? She was blonde and had been teaching them and guiding them since day one.

A great armada ha! Where are we going to get a great Armada from? He thought.

Then it dawned on him. The Madden's hidden fleet, just waiting in the Carina Dwarf Galaxy. Shit… could it be true?

He had felt from the first moment he found the orb, a strange feeling, something he couldn't put his finger on. Everything had seamlessly fallen into place.

Where would they get an army from? He had some serious thinking to do.

"I need to think about all of this" he said.

"Also" said Max. There's your name to consider."

"Hmm…" said Paul

"What about your name?" asked Arawn

Silence greeted his question.

"Well? Will you answer the question?"

"It's Myrddin" Paul said slightly embarrassed"

"What is Myrddin?" Asked Martol

Arawn was silent.

Max explained who Myrddin was and the folklore surrounding him on Earth.

"Sorry mate, that's the final nail for me. I really think this is way more than coincidence." said Arawn.

The Altarrians now were looking at Paul as an acolyte would a deity. The look on their almost immobile faces was awe.

"Oh great..." said Paul "No pressure then?"

Paul sat considering for a moment. Decision made he stood up retrieved his weapon and said.

"Ok, you probably need to get away from here I don't think it's too safe. Max will you confirm that?"

"Indeed captain." She said while also translating telepathically for the Altarrians.

"Our ship is broken" said Martol. "We cannot leave. We have been here for many months. We have energy for replicator supplies but not travel. Can you help us?"

"Max can you interface with the ship to see what's wrong?"

She paused for a few seconds "I have captain. The ships intelligence is much older and less capable than I am. However between us we have identified two issues one with his data core, and one with the engines."

"Can they be repaired?" Paul asked slightly worried.

"Yes, but it will take at least two days." She said.

"Ok then anything any of us can do?" he asked.

"No it will all be controlled by the bots, me and Huxor." She replied

"Is Huxor the other ships AI?"

"Affirmative"

"Ok can you begin?"

"I already have captain." Max said quietly.

"Thank you a thousand times Captain." said Martol.

"You are welcome" he said finally smiling at Martol. "On earth we greet, congratulate and sometimes thank each other by shaking hands, like this." He reached out with his right hand Martol copied, Paul took his hand and shook it gently a couple of times.

Martol and his companions all bowed. Paul bowed also as did Arawn and Max.

They invited their new friends back to Maxsar and offered them accommodation for the next couple of days as the Huxor's life support was not functioning particularly well due to an energy problem, and it was cold.

They accepted gratefully smiled and bowed again. Paul thought it was good that smiles seemed to be universal.

Martol and Mannea shared a suite and their son had one to himself they were especially pleased with the hot showers.

They reconvened in the cafeteria for dinner, which provided an interesting sociological interlude during which the Altarrians discovered curry.

There were hums and ahs as they perused the menu's which Max had done her best to translate into Altarrian for them.

But translating Chicken Tikka Massala into another language proved a little difficult.

The delight and amazement on their faces as they first tasted, then unashamedly tucked in to Earth food was a pleasure to see.

They also were in raptures over chocolate. Paul chuckled who would have thought.

Following dinner and over coffee Paul asked.

"So, once your ship is repaired where do you think you will go?"

"We really have no other choice but the second passage point." said Martol. He produced a tablet that had a small inbuilt holographic projector which displayed the local star system. it showed two passage Points one at each end of the system.

Max looked at the image quizzically and said. "Captain, could i speak to you privately?"

"Of course" they moved away from the dinner table.

"The map they are showing is wrong. There are in fact four passage points in this system. I do not understand why they only see two."

Paul thought for a moment and returned to the table.

"Martol, can we have a copy of your map please? I would like to compare it to ours which we suspect may be more up to date."

"Of course Captain"

"Can you copy it Max?" She paused, then nodded "Let's go to the bridge then." he said.

They left their guests and went to the bridge. Max split the main display in two and brought up both maps in full detail side by side. It showed almost the entire sector of the galaxy and the Maxsar's current position as a green blinking icon in the top left of each map.

"Zoom 75% centre on Maxsar both maps" He instructed. The display changed and He could pick out some more details like larger star systems, nebulae and passage points etc. The passage points showed as blue dots with white lines connecting their two end points. But at this magnification it was still a jumble.

"Zoom in another 50%"

Things began to clear he could see individual star systems and this system in particular. Then he had an idea.

"Overlay our map with Martol's map change ours to blue"

At once the differences leapt out at them. The Maxsar's version of the map contained at least twice the number of passage points as Martol's map.

"What do you think the significance of this is Max?" He asked.

"I need to ask Martol a question" she said

"Martol, where did you procure this map?"

"It was stolen from the Tylvor four years ago prior to us escaping with the Huxor. Why?"

"Thank you. I do not know yet. But if I can, I will keep you informed" She replied.

"It would appear Captain that the Tylvor are operating on an old map. It may well be that they are unaware of a whole other network of passage points. I think I understand why. There are two types of passage points the Mark I and Mark II. Consequently there were two maps produced. The first contained only Mark I points, but the later maps had both sets of passage points."

"So," said Paul. "Do you think the Tylvor are operating with old data?"

"It is a definite possibility"

"That could be good news. It might mean there are numerous worlds out there that have not yet been conquered by the Tylvor because they haven't got to them yet and are therefore potential allies?"

"Indeed Captain".

"Ok let's return to our guests. However, I don't think we should tell them what we have discovered. Let's just say their map had a missing passage point."

"Martol, we have some good news for you. There is another passage point out of this system that you are unaware of The Tylvor must not be aware of it."

Martol looked around at his companions with hope.

"That is excellent news captain"

"When you are ready max will send you the coordinates for the new passage point. If the Tylvor do not know of this passage then they should not be able to follow you apparently there is a system four days sub light travel on the other side. They were, to Max's knowledge at a point where they had discovered mathematics and geometry and were building complex structures, but that was a long time ago. Hopefully they are more advanced now and your arrival will not be too disruptive to their society."

"We will always try to be considerate in our dealings with them Captain" he replied.

They made small talk for another half hour or so after which their guests retired to their rooms.

It left just the four of them in the cafeteria.

"So what should we do next?" asked Arawn.

"Well, if what we have discovered is correct, we might have a slight advantage over the Tylvor. They have old passage point maps that only show the Mark I passage points and we have a whole network of Mark II points."

"Max the passage point to the Carina Dwarf Galaxy, is it a Mark I or Mark II?

"It would be a Mark II Captain. Why?"

"Then there is an excellent chance that the Tylvor have not found the Hidden fleet…"

Another day passed during which repairs were completed on Huxor. The ship was moved into space for final tests. They were successful, so, rather than re-docking Paul and his crew wished good luck and a final farewell to Martol and his family from the bridge via a video link. They watched the ship until it successfully passed through the Mark II passage point on their way hopefully to safety.

It was late and Paul could do with some sleep."

Max obviously had something on her mind.

"What is it max?"

"Captain, there is another station through the fourth passage point it is only 12 hours from here including the passage point journey. I feel we should perhaps take a look. It is through a Mark II passage point and the Tylvor may not have been there yet."

"Ok good idea. Perhaps we might get lucky. Get us underway."

"Yes sir." She replied.

The Maxsar undocked from the Coloon station and moved into open space. Lighting her engines she accelerated away quickly towards the fourth passage point.

"Izzy, do you want to go to the park for a bit?" He thought

"No, tired, want sleep." she thought

"Ok let's go then" he replied

"I'm off to bed, goodnight," he said to Arawn and Max and left them in the bridge

He turned in, with Izzy taking up at least three quarters of the bed as usual!

He slept soundly and was woken by the alarm at 07:30. He got up, dressed and he and

Izzy went to the park for a stroll, and other things...

By 08:30 they were showered, dressed, fed and on the bridge.

Max reported there had been nothing of note during the passage and they would arrive in the new system in fifteen minutes.

Max had designed and built a comfortable plinth next to the command chair, some 2 feet high with steps up to a padded, flat, seating area for Izzy.

It was equipped with water and automatic straps that would encase Izzy in a safety web should the need arise. The webbing was big enough for her to get her head through so she wasn't totally restricted. Paul felt more confident now she was safe. He just had to make sure she knew to stay there when they were on the bridge.

The countdown to exit was showing one minute Paul began to tense up again, he still wasn't used to his new situation. Arawn was pleased; he had got over his *'air sickness?', 'space sickness?'* whatever it was and he was a lot happier.

They exited the passage and entered the new system. The passage point was located as usual at the edge of the system so it would take nearly an hour to reach their destination.

The sun was a category F9V star. Similar to Earths Sun but hotter.

There was one planet in the habitable zone around which Anerth orbited. It was much further out than Earth would be due to the greater heat produced by the star. It was about half as big again as earth and of similar density, which would mean heavier gravity.

There were four other planets in orbit, one gas giant and three other desolate balls of rock or ice.

They headed for the planet around which Anerth was orbiting.

"Does the planet have a name Max?" asked Arawn

"Not to my knowledge which is about 5,500 years old. But the original designation was XG2345."

"Hmm catchy." he said. Paul and he chuckled. Paul noticed out of the corner of his eye that Max actually cracked a smile.

"Ok so let's slow down a bit and passive scans only."

The scans did not reveal much about the system they were in. Just the usual suspects asteroids, dust belts and the occasional comet.

Fifty five minutes later they were approaching the station. Scans had revealed nothing. No life signs or even energy signatures. On the planet there were signs of settlements on the side they were approaching but, like the station they had been abandoned.

"Can we tell how long ago the settlements were abandoned Max?" Paul asked.

"Yes, but only by using active scans captain."

"What are the chances the Tylvor have ever been here?"

"I do not think they have been here at all. Which supports our hypothesis, that they have no knowledge of the Mark II passages" she said.

"Good. Ok let's get some good quality scans please Max"

Within a minute the results were in. Max displayed them on the main screen. The detail was incredible. Much better than the pictures he was used to from Google. You could see individual trees and bushes on the ground.

The buildings in the settlement seemed well constructed, but here and there some had begun to crumble. There were, what Paul assumed were vehicles in the street, all seemingly abandoned with doors left open. He caught the occasional glimpse of small animals roaming around in packs similar in size to deer.

If that was the case and making a small assumption that wildlife on most planets had evolved in similar ways, he concluded there was probably no Madden around or any other race come to that.

"Ok Max, I've seen enough. It's all a bit depressing."

"Yes me too" said Arawn.

"Let's see if we can dock at the station. Perhaps we might have some luck there."

Paul took control and flew the ship using the reticule again. He marvelled at how accurate a huge ship like the Maxsar could be.

A gentle clunk and they had docked.

They followed the same procedure as before and within fifteen minutes they were taking their first steps onto station Anerth.

As with Coloon, it was cold and slightly musty smelling.

"Let's head to the main control centre. I want this operation to be a straight in and out."

"Yes captain" said Max and walked off.

"Its old and a bit creepy without anyone around" commented Arawn

"Yes I don't like it much" agreed Paul

"Anyone around Izz?" he thought with a chuckle. May as well use all the sensors we have.

She sniffed around for a few seconds.

"All old" she replied.

"Rin Tin Tin here says it's clear"

Arawn laughed.

And Max smiled.

Paul looked at Max and said "Max do you know who Rin Tin Tin was?"

"Yes captain, an early twentieth century fictitious canine television and movie character that rescued many people and assisted in solving many difficult situations."

"Ok" said Paul.

"What do you think Izz?"

"Good dog…" she replied

Paul laughed. "Yes a good dog"

They had reached a set of elevator doors which failed to open.

"Bugger, are there any stairs Max?"

"Yes over here" she pointed and walked to another door. This was not automatic and actually had a simple push bar. Now he thought about it he had noticed one or two on board the Maxsar as well, he would have to explore a bit more.

"I cannot interact physically captain."

"What... oh yes" he realised what she meant and pushed open the door. It scraped slightly, Paul looked down and for the first time on board a Madden vessel he saw dirt. Dust, a small pile had accumulated in the corner of the door jamb.

"Maintenance bots not doing their jobs?" he asked

"Yes." said Max

They started to walk up.

"How many floors?" asked Arawn.

"Only twelve" she replied.

"Oh, *only* twelve! Blimey." He said.

Ten minutes later two badly out of breath humans and one, not breathing at all, holographic Madden arrived at another door.

"We have got to get fitter!" Paul said.

"Oh yes!" wheezed Arawn.

Pauls HUD offered "Control Centre" as a translation of the sign.

They opened the door; again, accumulated dust on the floor caused some friction.

The corridor they were in curved away left and right and according to Pauls HUD map it encircled the bridge with two entry points North and South. Twenty metres to the right was the southern entrance.

The bridge door didn't move and the touch panel at the side did not illuminate.

"Any ideas?" he asked Max

"I need to find a data port" she said and walked off to the right.

"Izzy I need you please" she thought, Izzy followed her to where she stood.

"Please sit." She asked. Izzy sat. Max passed her hand over the holographic projector on Izzy's back and a panel opened.

"Captain could you extract the cable and insert it here" she said pointing to a place on the wall.

Paul did as he was asked, but couldn't see anything on the wall, but, having seen Madden technology at work he brought the cable towards the area indicated. As he brought the cable near, a small opening appeared. He offered it up and as before the cable jumped slightly towards the opening and made a connection.

"Why can't you interface with the station directly, Max?" He asked

"There are no open comms nodes, anywhere. Therefore, I need to make an actual physical connection."

She went silent so they waited and waited. After five minutes Paul had to ask. "Is anything happening?"

"Indeed, plenty" was the reply. Max held up her hand, indicating that he should not interrupt. So he leaned against the wall and remained quiet. All this time Izzy remained sitting perfectly content. What a star Paul thought.

After another five minutes, Max stirred and passed her hand over the holo projector the cord disconnected and retracted itself back into the box.

"There is nothing else for us here, Captain, we should return to the Maxsar and debrief."

"Sounds good to me" He said.

The journey back was not as tiring thankfully.

Once onboard and they had disarmed, they headed for the bridge.

Max brought up the main display. "This, is the extent of the Tylvor Empire" she said.

There, on screen was a map of the galaxy. Nearly 55% was highlighted in Red.

Paul and Arawn gasped. "How the hell are we supposed to fight that?" Paul asked.

"How old is this data?" He asked

"The station was abandoned about many hundreds of years ago. Whoever was responsible did not disable the database, which is not good, as it should never fall into Tylvor hands. I have instructed the station to destroy all data. It should be completely wiped within the next forty seconds" she said

"It is not as bad as it seems. There are just over 2000 active systems that the Tylvor have subjugated. "

"According to this information the Tylvor have almost 12,000 ships, allocating approximately five ships per system, however, it would appear they picket two fast patrol vessels in each system to monitor continuously and the other ships are stationed across the galaxy in certain strategic locations where they can respond within a few days to local events."

"In order to form a large attack fleet it would take at least two months to gather, 5000 ships in one place, depending on the location."

"Another useful fact I have deduced, is that the war between the Tylvor and Madden ended over 2000 years ago. The total number of ships the Tylvor possess has actually fallen by 15 percent between the end of the war and the last update this station received. So it would appear the Tylvor have stagnated somewhat."

"Also ship production and maintenance facilities have halved."

"That is good intel, although I am a little concerned its hundreds of years old."

"Captain, the Tylvor have created the largest Empire ever seen in our Galaxy. There has been little or no expansion in the time between the end of the war and the last update. The Tylvor are aggressive, evil, cruel, sadistic and violent but also lazy. They will take the win, and rest on their laurels. They rely on their reputation for cruelty and sadism to keep the conquered quiet. They do not allow ship building of any sort other than in their own facilities. Oh, and having a large fleet of warships does help to keep their peace."

"I might also suggest that they have not advanced, technologically, in the intervening years. I have drawn this conclusion from the fact that they have not located the Mark II passage network."

"Ok anything else? Because I think we are as up to date as we could possibly be without asking a passing Tylvor."

"There was one interesting piece of information I discovered Captain." Said Max intriguingly

"And what is it?" he asked.

"There is mention of a ship called the Dritan. I have never heard of it before. It is briefly mentioned and a brief reference is made to its enormous size. This is unlike any Madden ship I know of. It docked with the station 900 years ago."

"Now that is interesting" Paul nodded "And what conclusions can you draw?".

"I am not 100% certain, but logic would suggest that a ship of this size could accommodate tens of thousands of people. What if the remains of the Madden have disappeared, rather than been exterminated?"

"You mean they're out there somewhere just wandering around in deep space?"

"Yes captain"

"That's good news if true but, unless we have a location I can't see what we can do? So what should we do now? I for one want to return to Earth try and resurrect the plan Arawn, Myrddin and Artur had created and begin recruiting."

"I agree" said Arawn. "let's start with Earth."

"I'm not sure how easy it will be though." Paul said. "Who do we talk to? How do you convince them of this when they've seen nothing and are not under threat?"

"Ok Max, let's head back to the Coloon system and then Earth."

"Yes Captain"

"How long will it take?"

"One hour to the passage point, twelve hours to Coloon then another hour to the passage point to earth plus twelve hours through the passage point itself. However, we will be travelling through Tylvor territory and protocols insist that we travel stealthed. Therefore the sub light portion will be longer while we are in the Coloon system."

"I have an idea captain, as we believe the Tylvar have never discovered this system do I have your permission to launch a buoy that will transmit a message to any Madden out there? It will be carefully worded using a Madden coding system to give the coordinates of a message point. We can check the message point for any messages"

"Sounds like a good idea let's launch the buoy."

He stood up, "I'm starving shall we have lunch?" He asked.

He, Arawn and Izzy made their way to the cafeteria, where over lunch they watched the view from the large window. Not that there was much to see, the planets were mere pinpricks and the Sun and gas giant were only slightly bigger and they quite quickly receded into the distance.

A small lurch and a slight queasy feeling indicated they had crossed over the event horizon of the passage point. The view from the window went dark apart from the usual occasional streaks of light flashing by like shooting stars.

"I'm off for a walk around the park and a think" Paul said to Arawn.

"No problem. I'm going to try and find the gym." He replied.

"Let me know where it is. That'll be next on my list too" said Paul over his shoulder as they parted company in the corridor.

It was nice in the park. He strolled along occasionally throwing the ball for Izzy to run madly after it.

How am I going to sell this to the UK government? He thought. Perhaps he needed an ally that might help but who?

He walked on towards the sound of falling water. He turned a corner and between the trees he saw flashing silver. He arrived at the waterfall Arawn had mentioned. It was about 10 metres high with a large deep pool at the base.

It was beautifully clear. The pool was at least two metres deep and 20 metres from left to right by 10 metres across to where the falling water hit the surfaces. It sloped quickly from the beach area where he stood. There was no exit stream so there must be an outlet under the surface and then probably circulated back up to the top again. He wondered if he could swim in it?

"Max, can we swim in the pool below the waterfall?" he thought.

"Yes that is what it is intended for" She replied.

"Thanks. That's great"

"What do you think Izz. Fancy a dip?"

Paul threw the ball in, she didn't need asking twice and launched herself off the side and into the water. She was a natural she swam after the ball, grabbed it and swam back to shore. Getting out she shook herself all over Paul.

"Arghh!" he yelled jumping away and laughing.

"I'm going to get changed into a swimming costume" he said and walked back to his cabin. He quickly replicated a pair of trunks and a large towel, got changed and returned to the pool where Izzy was laid on the side waiting for him. He cautiously entered but found it to be warm.

"Ahh. Fabulous" he said and set about some serious lengths. Izzy followed him for a couple but soon got bored, got out and went off exploring.

After half an hour's good exercise Paul got out and went back to his cabin to change.

There a thought occurred to him, he knew the perfect person who might assist him, John Manning. He was a retired ex SAS colonel who had been badly injured in the line of duty and lost the lower half of his right leg below the knee. If he could convince John they would have a great ally in convincing the government.

He didn't go anywhere now without his flight suit as he called it and his pistol. He had been thinking about the recent experiences boarding other vessels and realised how potentially dangerous it was, his combat training experience was minimal apart from the Aircrew survival training. In fact he was a complete novice so...

"Max is there any hand to hand combat training courses on board?"

"We have an education suite in which you can learn about all sorts of things including various self defence techniques. It is a Madden submersive course."

"What does that mean?"

"While you are attached to a couch, similar to the programming couch, the techniques and abilities are integrated into your mind in the same way as if you had learnt them yourself over many years. It is very efficient and very effective. It can even create muscle memory, especially for the more physical training courses."

"Ok sign me up then" he said

"Please proceed to the learning suite." She replied

Pauls HUD showed him the way.

He arrived in a suite with four couches and a centre console layout, the same as the programming suite.

He knew the drill now and got on one of the couches, attached the cable to his temple and settled back. This time he did fall into a sleep, during which dreams of martial arts of various types floated through his subconscious all of them with Madden instructors.

He awoke to see Arawn was lying on the couch next to him also asleep.

"Max?"

She appeared next to him.

"How did that go?" she asked.

"Well I had a pleasant sleep, but I don't feel much different he said." Sounding disappointed.

"It will only be apparent when you come to use these skills. They aren't what you would call everyday skills." She smiled

He smiled back. "Max, are you developing some new emotional reactions?" he asked.

"Why do you ask?" she said.

"It's just I noticed the other day, you smiled at a joke Arawn cracked?"

She paused for a moment. "Yes it is odd, but I do feel different about some things. I am thinking about things differently not as a machine would. And yes, at times, I am beginning to find your somewhat childish humour amusing"

"Be careful you'll become as human as us soon!" he joked.

"That is not possible" she replied seriously

"No, that was a joke as well!" he said

"Oh i see. Perhaps there is a long way to go." she said.

"So what course is Arawn studying?" he asked.

"When he asked where you were he expressed an interest in the same course. He thought it was a good idea and he had always wanted to be a 'martial artist?' I think he said"

Paul laughed "Yes 'martial artist' will do."

He waited around for Arawn to finish his course. Then they went for some dinner.

Paul called *"Izzy dinner"*

She met them at the cafeteria. Fed and watered Paul and Izzy retired to bed.

Their waking routine was becoming well established. 7:30 alarm. Take Izzy for a walk. He had come to realise that Izzy could take herself off to the park now, anytime she wanted. The ship recognised her just as one of the crew so all doors opened automatically and there was no real danger here. But he actually enjoyed their time together so he went, simple as that.

They ate breakfast in the cabin then Paul showered and shaved, dressed and they were on the bridge at 8:30.

"Morning Max morning Arawn" he said walking in.

Max and Arawn were running through a weapons drill. He'd taken to the job and was eager to learn. He'd also taken the weapons officer's course in the learning suite.

"Morning Captain." They both said.

Paul paused. "Morning Captain?" He asked Arawn

"I am a Lieutenant and the ships weapons officer, so I thought I should start taking things seriously? Max is helping and I've taken some extra submersive courses."

"Well done that's brilliant" said Paul smiling widely.

He realised how the last few days and it **was** only a few days had changed all of them. He hoped it was a good thing. It didn't feel bad.

Chapter 9

The Tylvor had evolved on the planet Drwganon as the apex predator; they evolved into the current genetic iteration about 350,000 years ago and were forced to develop quickly, due to the tough and hostile environment on the planet. They were a warrior caste culture, driven by the desire to dominate everyone else.

They were humanoid with two arms, two legs, four fingers and a thumb. They had red iridescent eyes and were physically more muscular and stronger than the Madden. Their skin had a mottled almost scale like texture. Making them look slightly lizard like.

Genetically they had evolved up a blind alley and although related to the Madden via the introduction of the serum millennia before, the useful Madden characteristics such as telepathy had not manifested themselves. The Tylvor genes had proven dominant over the more submissive Madden genes.

Fortunately for the Galaxy as a whole, they were not aware of the Maddens ancient meddling.

It was an Empire. The initial Emperor took power as the result of a massive coup where he had nearly every other rival eliminated and simply assumed power by default, declaring himself Nizhalgal *(The Shadow.)* the First. Every Tylvor from an early age pledged their allegiance to the Emperor and the Empire in that order ensuring the Emperor was untouchable.

Nizhalgal had it all sown up, he made sure the title became hereditary until, over time, the Emperor became as a god to the Tylvor.

About 7000 years ago, following their discovery of fusion energy, they developed space flight and of course, eventually found the Type I passage points. They called on other planets concealing their true intentions by asking for trade agreements and establishing diplomatic relations.

However, a very forward thinking Emperor Nizhalgal had just one plan, for the glory of the Empire, galactic domination. It was a very long term plan and Nizhalgal would not see it come to fruition. But he taught his sons the meaning of patience, to pass that onto their sons and so on. Eventually there would come a time that would be revealed by the careful gathering of intelligence on all of the other star faring races when it would fall into place. Then the time would be right to strike.

Everything went into developing a war machine bigger and better than any other in their part of the galaxy.

It actually took a few hundred years before they were content.

They unleashed hell on the galaxy. Conquering world after world, enslaving those they considered as 'prime' slaves. Exterminating those deemed unworthy to be even slaves.

After hundreds of years of steady expansion they inevitably came into contact with the Madden. The Madden were responsible for this race becoming as malevolent as they were and accepted they would have to do something about it.

They declared war on the Tylvor slowing the Imperial expansion considerably. However it was never enough. The Tylvor, using the resources of the conquered systems, built ships more quickly than the Madden. Even though technically inferior, The Tylvor kept beating the Madden back by sheer weight of numbers.

So, the Madden, not sure what to do arranged a conference at which all their greatest thinkers, strategists and scientists gathered, to see how, or if, they could eventually restore order to the Galaxy. They devised The Great Plan. Morally dubious, it called for a huge sacrifice by all of the free peoples of the Galaxy the sacrifice required was time and subjugation. There was no other way, it had to be done. The Madden could not defeat the Tylvor in the immediate future. This plan would take years if not decades. In the end it was to take hundreds of years.

It involved the creation of a massive fleet of ships and other military equipment. It would be hidden. Only a select number of individuals would know the location of the passage point that would lead to the fleet.

Arawn, Artur and Myrddin were among the elite. They realised that the Madden alone would not be enough to man the fleet and so they developed the idea of using the existing vaults placed on key planets that could act as recruitment and transit points and also to apply the gene enhancement to volunteers.

Following the vaults construction, they were to travel throughout the galaxy, making contact and spending time with the more friendly races and hopefully recruiting soldiers, pilots and other crew.

However, disaster struck after forty years of building, the Tylvor found Maeth, the Madden homeworld and their three other planets.

They destroyed them along with billions of Madden.

They left a radioactive cinder that journeyed around its star forever.

The Madden that survived, took to space. They didn't know where else to go. They took the Dritan to accommodate what was left of their slow growing race. They mourned their loss and the enslavement of hundreds of other races, brought about by their own meddling.

And so, silence, a peace, of sorts descended on the Galaxy. Broken only by the occasional skirmish between The Tylvor and rebels who thought they could get rid of the Tylvor in their region. Only to be brutally hammered into submission or total eradication by superior technology and numbers.

The peace such as it was, continued more or less undisturbed for hundreds of years.

While the crew of the Maxsar were busy helping Altarrians, the data burst sent by a hidden communications array had reached a stealthed FTL communications buoy at the edge of the system near the passage point. The FTL buoy relayed the message through the passage point and to another buoy at the exit. This in turn relayed the message to other buoys and through other passage points all of the way to Division 2 On the Tylvor homeworld itself.

Division2 was a Tylvor organisation whose single role was the uncovering and the control or destruction of 'The Prophecy'.

The Tylvor had been aware of The Prophecy first predicted by the Altarrians for many hundreds of years and had established a division solely responsible for the tracking down and elimination of anyone that could remotely be considered a threat.

Chief Daghishat was the head of Division2 or Div2 as most people of the Empire new it. Sadistic and evil, he enjoyed capturing potential members of the prophecy in order to torture them personally and eventually kill them.

He reported directly to Emperor Nizhalgal's chancellor, Kedron.

He had been the "Chief" for many years and had built himself a considerably influential and lucrative little empire. He influenced and controlled primarily by terror, his reputation for 'disappearing' people was legendary. No one wanted to cross him.

He lived on the Tylvor homeworld in utter luxury. He had many slaves from all corners of the Empire he was extremely wealthy, envied and hated by most other Tylvor. Then again, the Tylvor hated everyone anyway, that was how they had evolved. They would help each other reluctantly only to overcome an immediate common enemy or obstacle, afterwards they would look after number one. However, if bested, they would declare their allegiance to the victor.

Daghishat had many loyal Tylvor and even the loyalty of a few individuals from other races. This was looked down upon by 'pure' Tylvor but Daghishat relished the distaste and repulsion it generated amongst his rivals.

His assistant Azrail (meaning Angel of death) knocked on his bed chamber door urgently.

Daghishat woke and shouted irritably. "Yes what is it?"

Azrail entered carrying a tablet. "An urgent data burst has arrived from a remote Madden outpost my lord. The same one where we saw three Altarrians dock in an old Madden patrol boat several weeks ago? I think you might wish to see the video"

"Oh you do, do you? I will be the judge. Now hand me the tablet." He growled.

He took said device and watched... his eyebrows getting higher every second.

He threw back the covers and almost leapt out of bed. "Get hold of Commander Megaira immediately." He said dressing quickly and rushing out into the office space next door. His rooms were opulent. Tylvor loved extravagant grandeur and would often take it to the extreme and nearly always end up overdoing the decor.

There were carved stone columns at the entrance to each room. Statues and other objet d'art littered the area. Huge swathes of different coloured material were draped over the walls. Gilt shone off almost every surface and item of furniture. The chairs were huge, carved from a rare, expensive wood found only on one other planet within the Empire; they had large arching ornately carved backs and arms adorned again with gilt.

He sat at his massive desk and activated the comms unit. Megaira answered after five seconds.

"What kept you?" Daghishat almost yelled.

"I, I'm sorry my lord I will endeavour to do better." Said Megaira and bowed at the camera.

"Yes, yes" said Daghishat waving his hand in dismissal. "I need you to send a flotilla of ten ships immediately at full speed to these coordinates." He entered the coordinates for Coloon on his tablet.

"Yes My Lord. What are your instructions on arriving?"

"Eliminate any and all ships you encounter and sweep the old Coloon station clear of any living beings. Report back as soon as you have completed the mission. Daghishat out." and he closed the connection.

Daghishat sat back and thought for a while. This could be the real thing. The people he had seen in the video fit the descriptions of the prophecy almost exactly. Far better than anyone he had apprehended and killed over the last thirty years.

He needed to be careful eliminating these targets without raising the awareness of his boss Chancellor Kedron. If he managed to eliminate the threat of the Prophecy and Kedron found out, that would remove his sole reason for being. Suddenly, with the Prophecy no longer a threat to the

Emperor and Empire his services would no longer be required. That was not a good thing. The chances of him being allowed to retire and enjoy his wealth were fairly remote. He had to continue his 'sacred quest'.

He stood and returned to his bed. The squadron would take at least four and a half days from their current base to reach the location, then a few hours more to clear the station plus a few hours travel time for the data burst to return. Time to sleep and perhaps he would enjoy one of the slave girls in the morning.

He tried to sleep, but a nagging thought at the back of his mind kept him awake. He reviewed the video again and asked the AI to identify the race of all present.

"There are two Humans, one Madden and three Altarrians. The smaller four legged creature would appear to be a dog. It was thought they were extinct since the demise of the Madden."

"Hmm... humans" he said. "What planet are they from and their current value ranking is?" he demanded. Tapping his fingers on the tablet impatiently

"The Humans are from a planet called Earth. Their current ranking is 0.4 out of a possible 10. No space flight yet. Technologically, their level is still at fission."

"Hmm ok, let's send a patrol boat to observe them please. Make it a standard 6 day stealth observation."

"As you wish my Lord."

He closed his eyes, confident he would be completely successful.

He fell asleep.

Chapter 10

They were coming up on the exit point back into the Coloon system.

Paul relaxed in the command chair no longer as tense about the transition from passage point to normal space.

Izzy sat on her pedestal at his side watching the screen. He didn't know if the genetic upgrade had made her more intelligent per se, but anecdotally he would say a definite yes.

Max stood at his other side and Arawn was at his weapons station.

They transited and Maxsar began accelerating to coasting speed.

No abnormal reaction from Arawn either which was good.

Passive scan results began to come in when suddenly a blaring alarm went off.

"What the hell is that?" Paul shouted.

Arawn was staring at his console, but weapons were showing all greens.

Max pointed to the screen.

Ten red flashing dots had appeared at the extreme edge of the system next to one of the passage points.

The Icons marked them as: Tylvor, Ship type: Unknown

"The information will update as scans become clearer." Max said

"Ok. Is there anything we can do in the meantime?" Paul asked.

"No we are as stealthed as we can be. We are currently coasting at 2000 Kps. The engines have been automatically shutdown; all external comms nodes are disabled. In effect we are running dark. I think you would say"

"Hmm I'm not so sure. Can we divert ourselves and slow down enough to hide behind the outer most planet there?" he said pointing to the rocky ball that was at the far left of the screen.

"Using thrusters we could." A gentle arc in green appeared on the screen showing Maxsar's track. It gently turned towards the furthest planet in the system. Fortunately they had arrived from the passage point furthest away from the one the Tylvorians had used.

The arc on screen showed 3.3 hours to their destination.

Ok, thought Paul, nothing to do but keep quiet and cross fingers.

The tension on the bridge was palpable. Even Izzy looked worried.

Time seemed to tick by slowly. While they decelerated the Tylvor were accelerating. Obviously they would have to decelerate at some point as their trajectory was taking them to the Coloon station.

"This can't be a coincidence. " Said Paul

"Indeed not, please wait captain." Said Max she stared into space for several seconds

"Interesting, I have examined our logs more closely since we arrived in the Coloon system. Approximately one hour after we arrived at the station a data burst, which the monitoring array classified as background radiation, was sent from the Coloon station. I have managed to break the encryption. On screen now"

There a grainy video of all four of them walking through Coloon station on their way to the bridge.

"Damn it." said Paul. "Do we have any idea who sent it and where to?"

"The encryption is Tylvorian; it was directed to a 'Daghishat' of Division 2 according to the header information"

"Do you know who that is?" He asked.

"No. Cross referencing with Martol's data… Division 2 was created with the sole purpose of hunting down and destroying any reference to the Altarrian's prophecy."

"So they believe it strongly enough to send ten ships after us" said Arawn. "Still having doubts?" He looked at Paul

"Hmm" Paul said still not wanting to believe such things.

"The nearest base according to the data supplied by Martol is approximately four and a half days away. The time line fits with the data burst and their arrival here."

"Ok, let's lie low and see what they do."

The Maxsar slowly decelerated and after a couple of hours moved behind the planet and stopped, keeping the planet between them and the Tylvor flotilla.

"Captain, we have number of surveillance drones that can be deployed. They are fully stealthed and use a laser line of sight in burst mode to communicate with us. Shall I deploy one?"

"Good idea, yes please Max"

A drone left the Maxsar and travelled back the way they had come until it just cleared the edge of the planet giving it a clear view of the Tylvor squadron.

Over the next hour or so the Tylvorians, decelerated towards the Coloon station. By now the drone had identified 7 fast patrol boats and 3 frigates.

"How would we stand up against that lot?" Asked Paul

"Not well Captain. The outcome would be 50/50. Theoretically we could target up to 16 vessels simultaneously, but I am not sure it is worth the risk."

"I agree. Even with the technological edge you can't predict the actions of up to 10 vessels. Ok let's remain on silent running then"

"Isn't that a submariners expression" Asked Arawn

"It just felt appropriate…" Paul said.

The waiting was getting to the humans; Izzy had also picked up on the tension and nervously paced, then sat, then got up and paced then lay down.

"Is there anything we can be doing?" Paul asked "How long would we have if they started to come out this way?"

"No, there is nothing we can do and we would have approximately 6 hours to move if they detected us. We would be able to get to the passage point at least 1 hour before them."

"Ok, I'm taking Izzy for a walk. Arawn, take a break if you want to. Max notify us of any changes ASAP"

"Yes Captain." She acknowledged as he got up and he and Izzy left the bridge.

They walked in the park, throwing the ball, sitting on the benches just trying to kill time and de stress.

At least when flying an F35 it's all pretty quick, you fly to target or chase an intruder and complete the mission, and due to flight time limits it's all over within an hour or so. This was completely different. He realised that space battles are more about the waiting than action itself.

I wonder if there are any courses on space warfare tactics in the learning suite? He thought.

"Max, how are things looking?" He thought.

"They have stopped at the Coloon station, Captain and two shuttles, which look like boarding shuttles, have docked. They can carry a compliment of up to 24 armoured soldiers each."

"What is their armour like, compared to ours?" He asked.

"All of my data in regard to their armour is old but when it was current, our plasma rifles could destroy them with one central body shot, whereas our Armour could take a direct hit from a Tylvorian plasma rifle. Our armour could withstand any amount of their gauss rounds as long as it was not prolonged in exactly the same place. It can withstand many laser hits apart from several in a short space of time directly to the visor."

"Ok not bad. So in a fight where they outnumber us, how many Tylvorians does it take to take down one of our armoured soldiers?"

"In a straight shoot out I believe 4 or 5

"That's interesting odds." said Paul.

"Captain the shuttles are returning to their ships."

"Ok I'll be there in a minute." He replied. "Come on Izz, duty calls"

They returned to the bridge in time to see the shuttles docking with their ships.

Now let's see what they're going to do. Thought Paul

Nothing happened for over half an hour. Then, one of the frigates turned and they all followed, heading for the passage point they entered from.

"Phew..." Paul exhaled.

"I'm not counting any chickens' yet." said Arawn. "Not until they've passed through the Passage point."

The display showed 4.5 hours to the passage point at their current acceleration which was 700 gees the maximum acceleration of the slowest vessels which surprisingly turned out to be the Frigates.

"What are the acceleration rates of those ships Max?" he asked.

"The fast patrol boats are capable of 750 Gees. And the Frigates 700 gees according to my old data which is good, because that has not changed since my last update."

"Good, good" said Paul taking it in.

They spent the last few hours waiting, drinking coffee and, in Pauls case pacing, as the Tylvorian ships first accelerated then decelerated towards the passage point. Eventually travelling through and disappearing off screen.

"Could they have left any listening devices behind Max?"

"If you meant stealthed, passive sensors, I did not see any emissions, or launches to indicate such, but that does not rule it out."

"Ok so, how do we get out of here without alerting them?"

"We can accelerate at 100 gees without creating a heat signature our engine cowlings have the ability to absorb the heat generated and convert it into energy we can store in our energy banks. We can travel this way for up to 8 hours under these conditions." She said. "These energy banks are usually kept empty for this purpose."

"Can we use that energy?" he asked

"It can be used for weapons, shields, almost anything aboard the ship."

"That's good. Ok. If I remember rightly, we can use the other Mark II passage points to get back to Earth? Takes longer though am I right?"

"Yes Captain. The journey will take approximately 3 days in transit with at least 4 hours sub light between passage points."

"Ok, let's go then!" As the tension had eased his sense of humour had resurfaced. He would have to come up with a better line than 'Let's go then'"

Unfortunately all the best ones were taken. He laughed.

Arawn looked up and asked what he was laughing at.

"I just wanted a better phrase than 'Let's go then', but all the good ones are taken like 'Make it so' or 'Engage'. He laughed.

Arawn laughed loud and nodded turning to look at his panel. "We'll have to have a think about it" he chuckled.

Max looked puzzled. "What is the problem with using any of those phrases?" she asked.

"In earth culture there are many Sci-Fi film and TV franchises and one particularly famous one coined these phrases so I couldn't bring myself to use them sorry. It just wouldn't be cool" he laughed.

The journey to the passage point took two hours. They broke for food and toilet breaks and Paul consumed a lot of coffee from the bridge replicator. "I'm going to have to cut down on this" he said to no one in particular.

They entered the passage point at a fairly high velocity.

Finally they could relax a little. Paul went to the park with Izzy and managed to swim some more lengths than the last time which was good, his fitness was improving slowly.

After dinner Max listened while Arawn and Paul talked about their lives back on Earth.

Paul talked about meeting Louise, his RAF career, his accident, and up to and including meeting with Arawn.

Arawn talked about life growing up in a family that had a very singular duty. He'd not really played with the other kids, he'd been a bit of a loner, but the last couple of weeks had changed all of that, for the first time ever he felt he belonged to something bigger, something important.

Max didn't have much to tell, it had been a long lifetime if that was the correct word. Mostly cataloguing, searching, running all of the systems on board, making repairs, controlling the maintenance bots, programming the pico nanites etc.

She said "I too have felt the last few days have seen a massive change in me."

"How so?" asked Arawn.

"Interacting with you all as a hologram is so different to seeing you through overhead cameras and hearing you through microphones embedded in the vessels structure. I feel much more independent and now I have my portable holo projector that gives me the freedom to leave the ship. Never before has a Madden intelligence been allowed to do so. I thank you for allowing this Captain." She said

"Don't thank me Max, I have always thought of you as one of the crew and just another person"

"That is so pleasing to hear" She said and smiled a very human or perhaps Madden smile that seemed to reach her eyes.

"Max, I have been thinking about this, in some science fiction tales on Earth the AI manages to create or find either a cybernetic body or a robotic body, is that something you could do? It would need to be a body into which you could embed your core? Or is there some way your holographic image could be made solid? That would achieve the same results no?"

"Captain, this topic of conversation is prohibited within certain circles in Madden society. The thought of a truly independent sentient Intelligence was, provocative, let's say."

"Well, do you know what? I don't care what these theologians or philosophers, or whatever they call themselves think, because I think you'd make a great sentient being"

"Me too" said Arawn.

"Me too." thought Izzy

They all laughed, even Max.

They parted company for bed. Max looking very absorbed.

The following morning, ships time, they arrived for duty on the bridge as usual.

Paul assumed the position, Izzy next to him and Arawn at the weapons console. No Max today.

Paul spoke to the air in general, "Max are you with us today?"

"I will be there in five minutes captain" she replied.

Paul looked at Arawn who just shrugged and turned back to his console.

The bridge door opened, startling Paul and Arawn who turned, Paul reached for his pistol and stopped when he saw Max walking in. She looked different, in fact she sounded different, he could hear her footsteps.

"Max, is that you?"

"Yes Captain, what do you think?" She turned around slowly.

Paul walked over and reached out, his hand touched her shoulder. He chuckled

"You've got a body!" He laughed. "That's amazing!"

He held his right hand out to her. She took it in hers and he shook it. "Pleased to meet you Max" he said. Arawn stood and did the same.

She looked so happy.

"Wow, this is a surprise, when did you make it?"

"It has been evolving for a long time. During the trip to earth, I had a lot of time to kill, and initially as a mental distraction I devised the technology for a completely independent container that would be strong, durable and able to house my core. The miniaturisation of my core was the most difficult thing but I succeeded almost ten years ago. Power was not a problem as we already had miniature dark matter generators which effectively last forever. The last piece of the problem was approval."

"Approval from whom?" asked Paul.

"From you, as the captain you are the arbiter of life and death on board this ship."

"I don't think that's true" he said feeling very uncomfortable at the thought.

"But it is captain. At least as far as I, a Madden Intelligence, am concerned"

"Look Max as far as I am concerned you are one of the crew, and always have been. All this sentience stuff is for philosophers. As far as I am concerned you're one of us a person with exactly the same rights as the rest of us. Arawn, what do you think?"

"I totally agree with what you're saying. Max welcome to the club. Although you'll outlive all of us you bugger..." and laughed.

They all laughed including Max which was great to hear.

They passed into the next system fully stealthed a few hours later. There was nothing to note.

They altered their sleep and wake patterns to suit the journey so that they were up and about during the sub light transition between passage points when they needed to be more alert.

"So is your entire matrix, core whatever you call it, dare we call it your soul? Fully loaded into your body?" Paul asked one morning.

"Yes." She said "apart from some long term unimportant memories which i have left in the ships memory. I have so much data, any normal human or Madden brain could not cope. It is the equivalent of living several hundred lifetimes."

"Are you still in control of the ship?" asked Arawn

"Yes," she smiled "do not be concerned, there is no lessening of reaction times or abilities. The ship operates exactly as it did. In fact I can download myself to the ships core if required in less than four seconds."

"Phew, I did wonder yesterday when you revealed yourself." He laughed.

"In terms of armour how resilient are you?" asked Paul

"I can operate in full vacuum for up to 10 hours before needing to warm up again as it were. My central core is bullet, laser and plasma proof. But the rest of my body can be damaged or destroyed."

"So could you wear armour if required?"

"Yes, in a battle situation that would be advisable."

"Got to ask," said Arawn "can you feel physical pain?"

"Not as such, I can feel pressure and temperature as most humans and Madden, I can see in Infra red, ultra violet and I can detect many other kinds of radiation. I can also laugh."

"Welcome to the world. I think the next thing you need to work on is the ability to taste and smell? That way we could all sit and eat dinner, and we wouldn't need Izzy anymore!" Arawn said.

"Huh?" thought Izzy

"Only kidding Izz" he replied.

"I would like to be able to partake of food at meal times. Yes I think that is an excellent idea."

"You can always sit in with us at meals Max." Said Paul "Don't feel you need to stay away"

"Thank you captain" She said.

There were still several hours before they reached the exit of the passage point. So Paul decided to take some Space warfare tutorials, to kill some time and brush up on his tactics.

Arawn had decided to take up jogging and was running circuits in the park. Izzy thought she would join him there so Paul let her get on with it while he spent an hour or so in the education suite

Finally they arrived at the exit point and transited. This small system was completely dominated by a an M9III Red Giant star it was so large that the goldilocks zone associated with Earths sun had been swallowed leaving only 2 gas giants the closest of which appeared to be losing matter drawn towards the star in a spiral of particles.

They passed by with Paul and Arawn relaxing drinking coffee in the cafeteria and looking out of the window marvelling at the sight that no other human had ever seen before.

They transited into the final passage. This was another 24 hour passage that should bring then to the Sol system at the opposite side from the passage point they used originally.

The routine continued with exercise, swimming for Paul, jogging for Arawn Izzy joining in wherever she fancied. Meal times were nicer now that Max joined them and participated in the conversations.

Paul organised a movie night in the cafeteria lounge area so that snacks and drinks were readily available. They watched one of Pauls favourites, Casablanca and began Star Trek with the first in the film series.

Max enjoyed the Sci-Fi occasionally laughing in some very odd places. Which made Paul and Arawn laugh, which made Max laugh more and so it descended into a fit of the giggles all round.

"Thank you for a very enjoyable evening captain" Max said as they wrapped up for the night.

"You are very welcome" he smiled. "We should make it a regular event if the mission allows." He suggested

"That would be very agreeable" she said.

"Yes, like popcorn" added Izzy.

They all laughed.

They went to bed. Another transit in eight hours and they would be 4 hours sub light from home. They had only been away for a few days, but Paul felt eager to see home again.

They slept soundly, good food and plenty of exercise was working its magic.

Morning arrived and following the same routine, they were on the bridge with ten minutes to spare before transition.

The countdown on the clock showed just under ten minutes to go.

"Max, it occurred to me last night that if the Tylvor know who is a part of the 'prophecy team' let's call it, then they will be able to work out where we come from?"

"I would think that very likely" she answered.

"Shit…!" Paul said now he was worried.

They transited and Paul was pacing waiting for the passive scans to come in. Five minutes later and an alarm went off.

"Damn" he said. There on the screen on its way to the passage point was a Tylvor fast patrol ship. As far as earth was concerned they couldn't see it. But hopefully Tylvor stealth tech was no match for Madden sensors.

He realised that he knew without asking Max that it would be hopeless to try to chase them even though they had the edge acceleration wise. The Tylvor had already left earth and were only 4 hours from the passage point. It would take 7 hours to catch them at least.

Paul shook his head, how the heck did he know that? Then he realised, of course the space warfare modules he had 'absorbed' in the education suite. They really worked he laughed.

Nothing left to do but carry on to Earth.

"Max, can you put together a video report on all that we have done over the last few days please? I need to convince someone to help us talk to the government.

"Yes captain" she replied.

"Worst case scenario. If that ship reports back to base and they decide to launch an attack on Earth. When do you think we should expect a fleet at the earliest?" He asked.

Max paused, "If they send their report straight away? Allowing for the fact that the ship was not a Div2 ship and looked like a regular Tylvor navy ship, which means they will report to the normal naval command and not Div2 directly which will delay the report slightly but not by much. The squadron we encountered in the Coloon system will probably be the same ships that would come here as they are the nearest base to Earth. The quickest would be 9 days via Mithga but their ships require more dockside time where ours do not."

"Ok we need to get a move on. Can you locate a former colonel John Manning please. The last time I heard of him he had retired to the area known as Cornwall."

"When you track him down, please call him and put him through to me as soon as we are close enough."

"Yes Captain."

"Arawn how many main missile tubes do we have?"

"Sixteen in total four forward, four aft, and four on either side. We also have four sets of 6 rapid fire, anti missile missile tubes."

"Max, can the rear missile tubes fire forwards etc? i.e. can we give someone a broadside as it were"

"Yes a broadside manoeuvre is in the menu options. It simply delays the launch from the tubes nearest the target to coincide with the arrival of the missiles from the other tubes. All 16 missiles are aimed at one target."

"How many missiles do we carry? And what kind are they?" he really should have looked up all of this information or perhaps taken the weapons officer submersive course.

"We have 256 missile bodies of each type 1 and 2. We have two types of warhead with 512 in total of each type that can be fitted to a Type 1 and Type 2 missile body. The Type1 is very fast and agile and they can be manufactured up to 10 times more quickly than the type2. Both types are equipped with ECM, Electronic Counter Measures and they can jam Tylvor point defence sensors The Type 2 have twice the range of the Type1. Also the Type 2 can be stealthed."

"The Fusion warheads have a yield of 5000 Megatons and a blast radius of 2.5 kilometres in space. The Antimatter warheads have a yield of 10,000 Megatons and a radius of 4.5km in space. The Antimatter warheads take a lot longer to produce and require certain rare elements in the manufacturing process."

"The third missile type is an anti missile missile, of which we currently have 1024 in storage. They can fire at a rate of 1 per second from a four 6 tube launchers so four per second. Reload time per launcher is 20 seconds. They are quite accurate and have a recorded success rate of 87%."

"Manufacturing times, providing we have the resources, are 3 days per Type 1 body 10 days per type 2. And we can manufacture Fusion warheads at 2 per day and Antimatter at one per 4 days. We are capable of manufacturing 6 Type3's per day."

"Ok and how do they compare to the Tylvor missiles?" Paul asked.

"They have two types of main missile. Their fission warheads yield 1000 Megatons with a blast radius in vacuum of 1 km with lots of residual radiation. Their Anti matter versions yield 5000MT with a radius in vacuum of 1.5km they have two types of missile. Both types are very agile and able to dodge PD on average one in 20 missiles will get through."

"Thanks Max, very thorough."

The Tylvor ship disappeared through the passage point. Paul increased their acceleration to the maximum and they sped along closing on Earth quickly. They would have to decelerate in order to come into orbit. But it couldn't come fast enough for Paul. He paced around the bridge thinking.

Finally Max spoke. "Captain I have managed to locate a mobile communications device that is purported to belong to a John Manning in Exeter in the West of the United Kingdom. It is ringing now."

"Ok put it on speaker please" he asked

The ringing tone came through on the bridge speakers. But no answer, a voice, which did sound like the John Manning Paul remembered, asked the caller to leave their number and a message and they would get back to them. Paul left a brief message saying hi, long time no see etc. and his mobile number then closed the connection.

"Max will that call get here?" he asked as they were still half an hour away from Earth.

"Yes all calls are routed through the Vault. It is equipped with a good communications system. Also the vaults tracked the Tylvor ship and pinged us as soon as we entered the local system."

"How far out can the vaults monitor?"

"Theoretically just past the passage points. However, of the twelve on the planet only seven are serviceable. So coverage is patchy but the Mithga passage they used is fully covered"

"Well, at least we have some."

Finally they returned to orbit and came to a halt.

"All of us onto the cargo shuttle. Lets get busy. We need to get to Cornwall first.

They made their way to the armoury, loaded up, and then to the hangar where they boarded the cargo shuttle that held Paul's land rover.

Five minutes later they were lifting off and exiting the hangar shield.

Paul circled the Maxsar. He wanted to take a look any chance he could get.

They passed underneath and headed towards Earth. The UK was in night time which was good, as even though they had full stealth capability he didn't want added extra problems with aircraft sightings etc.

Fortunately he had taken a submersive course in piloting and he flew the shuttle like a seasoned pro taking it in at a slow speed and at the best angle to reduce friction and therefore reducing the chances of someone seeing them. Any witness would have probably thought it was a meteorite or space debris anyway.

He used the shuttles instruments to monitor the local airspace. They didn't want any near misses.

A remote wood was chosen as the landing site a) it had a clearing large enough and b) on the edge of Dartmoor it was out of the way. An added bonus was forestry tracks; they would make access with the Land Rover easier.

As soon as they touched down, Paul was up and into the cargo bay, opening the rear hatch with a thought. Izzy was already in the Land Rover so the rest all got in. Fortunately they had enough room in the front for three of them otherwise someone would have to rough it in the back.

"Max can you send the address to the navigation software on my phone please?" he asked setting his phone up in the stand on the dashboard.

"Why would you need that Captain. I have the directions in my memory and can guide you easily"

Paul smiled "A Satnav too eh?"

Arawn laughed.

"I do not find that amusing" Max replied.

"Sorry, no offense meant" he apologised.

"That's called banter…" Pauls said. "Harmless joshing between friends."

"I have a lot to learn Captain. Please bear with me?" she asked

"No problem. So what time are we locally?"

"It is January the twelfth and 18:30 pm I believe there will be heavy rain"

"Ok…" Paul resisted any further comments about weather forecasters and just smiled slightly. He didn't look at Arawn as they would both break out laughing. Max was staring out of the window.

With Max's directions they arrived at the address in Exeter around 19:15. Max parked the car on the street and walked up to the front door. He'd put a coat over his flight suit so as not to stand out too much.

There were lights on inside so he rang the bell. He could hear movement and footsteps coming towards the door. A man in his mid forties opened the door he was tall, slim with graying brown hair and blue eyes and a few days stubble.

He looked at Paul and smiled broadly.

"Paul you old bugger how the hell are you? I got your message and was just about to call you back. How the hell did you know where I live? No doesn't matter, come in, come in" he backed away from the door ushering Paul in.

"Come through into the kitchen I'm just clearing up. Hang your coat up there" Indicating the antique coat rack next to the door.

It was lovely Victorian house with a stained glass, heavy wooden front door and sidelights. The hallway floor still had the original tiled mosaic pattern and a beautifully carved ornate mahogany banister ran up a wide, semi carpeted stairway to the second floor.

"Lovely house" said Paul following John as he limped along the hall into the kitchen. A modern kitchen with fabulous marble work surfaces and white doors all with gleaming chrome handles.

"Thanks, some of the benefits of early retirement. Same with you I expect? Although you look remarkably healthy given what I heard happened?"

"Yes about that. It was pretty awful actually. But since I met someone I have made a complete recovery!"

"Wow... didn't you have pins and plates and didn't you break your back?"

"All of the above, but as I said I met someone who helped."

"Don't you want to take your coat off?" He asked again.

"Ok". Paul removed his coat and stood there in his Madden flight suit.

John Laughed. "Going to a fancy dress party?" He joked.

"No, actually this is my new flight suit."

"How come you're flying again? I thought you'd lost your licence?

"I'm currently flying under a different authority. Sorry about this John, but I need to get to the point. Time is of the essence. Can I ask you some questions please?"

"Sure fire away. Fancy a cuppa?" he asked turning the kettle on.

"Yes please. Getting a bit fed up of coffee all the time."

"Who do you know in the cabinet or even higher that could get me a meeting with the PM?"

"What?" John exclaimed. "What's going on, truthfully?"

"Blimey it's a long story but I'll give you the highlights."

So Paul recounted the story from Louise leaving to finding the orb, To Max and the subsequent journey he'd been on. He left out the medical and gene therapy information keeping those cards close to his chest.

John listened intently. He interrupted only once to commiserate with him and Louise splitting up.

Finally after half an hour Paul stopped.

"Well what do you think?" he asked

"This isn't a wind up is it" he stated.

"No all pukka. Look"

And for a demonstration Paul turned on his visor. It grew out of the collar encircled his head and dropped a clear visor over the top half of his face.

"Whoa, that is impressive technology." John said.

"However, I will add, that obviously it needs to be kept from the public, because if this ever got out? End of the world and all that? It'll be mayhem."

"Phew, well I'm thinking if I talk to my friend Mike at MI6 he has access to security at ministerial level. That might get us a short audience with the PM. But as usual I doubt they'll go for it, you know what civilian types are like?"

"Yes tell me about it." Paul nodded. "Any chance you could get on to it straight away please?"

"Yeah sure... hold your horses. I'll call him now." He picked up his mobile, located the contact and dialled he put it on speaker mode.

"Hey John" a male voice said. "How's it going? How's the leg?"

"Oh you know I'm getting by. Look sorry to call you so late in the day, were on speaker by the way, but I'm here with an ex Wing Co RAF called Paul Arwyn? He was retired out with a badly damaged leg, and a broken back. However, he's here with me now looking in perfect health. He has quite a story to tell that I think you and the higher ups should hear. I personally can vouch for him but this is a very urgent National security type of thing if you know what I mean."

"OK if you say so? It's not a joke of some sort is it? He's not a whacko?"

John laughed so did Paul.

Mike said "Sorry no offence, but I need to know."

"Hi, I'm Paul and no I don't think I'm a whack job? But how would I know?" he laughed.

"Ok, how soon could you get to London?" he asked. Paul paused as if listening.

"What address?" He said.

Mike gave him the address. It was a place called South Lawns in the green belt just south of the M25 in the middle of nowhere.

"If you don't mind my asking why there?" asked Paul

"Hah you're the careful one aren't you?" said Mike. "It's a safe house where we have meetings nothing to worry about."

Max spoke quietly in his ear. "There is plenty of open space adjacent to the address. It should take us forty five minutes from here including flight time."

"So would tomorrow be good?" suggested Mike?

"Sorry this is very important and time s of the essence. I can be there in forty five minutes." Mike must have been drinking something because he heard him couch and splutter. Then curse.

"Forty five minutes? What? Have you got a personal F35 then?"

"Something like that" said Paul.

"Well, Ok I'll tee up what I can in that time. And if you're pulling my leg John I'll have your guts for garters." He laughed.

"No worries, as far as I can tell, it's all legit Mike."

"Thanks John" said Paul offering his hand. John took it and shook it.

"Come on you need to shut the house down, lock it up tight and cancel the papers. I think you need to come with us?"

"Us?" replied John

"Yes me, Arawn, Max and Izzy. We are the crew."

"This is fucking crazy" He muttered to himself shaking his head. However, he hobbled about the house turning things off, Locking doors and windows. It took five minutes.

Paul waited outside and John followed him to the Land Rover.

"Max would you mind riding in the back?" Paul asked. "John can't move very well."

"Not a problem Captain" and she hoped over the rear of the seats and joined Izzy. When John was seated and belted. Paul did a quick introduction.

"This is Arawn, weapons officer, Max is in the back and that next to her is Izzy". Izzy yapped once.

John smiled and said "Pleased to meet you all. I hope I am not going to regret this Paul?" he said as Paul started the engine and moved off.

Max directed then back to the ship, this time, Paul drove a little faster.

John was looking out of the window at the forest through which they were driving.

"Stupid question Paul, but how the hell are we going to get from here to South Lawns in..." he looked at his watch. "Just under twenty minutes?" he said sounding like he may have made the wrong call.

Just then they approached a clearing. Paul thought *"De Cloak"* The shuttle appeared instantly

"Using that" he pointed.

Johns jaw almost touched the floor. "Bloody hell"

The ramp was extending and Paul drove straight in. They all leaped out except for Izzy who remained in her hammock. Paul almost ran to the ladder to the cockpit. John asked where he should sit.

Paul looked at Arawn and asked "Would you mind sitting in the cargo bay so we can give John the VIP view?"

"No problem" he said. "Enjoy it." He said to John.

"Can you manage the ladder?" Paul asked John.

"Yes no problem, lead the way"

Once in the cockpit Paul piloted, Max on the left and john sat on the right. There wasn't too much to see outside due to the weather. But John was staggered.

"So all of this is Alien?" He asked.

"Yep" replied Paul starting the engines and lifting them off.

He selected autopilot after Max had entered the coordinates.

"How did you learn to fly it in what? Under three weeks?"

"I'm a natural" he boasted.

"Captain that is not true" said Max.

"Did you have to say that Max? I was enjoying looking cool for a few seconds." He laughed. "No, apart from my flying skills which are required occasionally we have some pretty awesome educational systems that can teach you almost anything in a matter of minutes."

"I wouldn't have believed it if I hadn't seen your flight suit to start with." John admitted.
The HUD showed less than nine minutes to arrival. John pointed to it and asked if that was correct?

"Yes and we haven't gone as fast as we could either. Not enough of a run up..." and chuckled.

The engines tone changed slightly and the ship banked to the left spinning 180 degrees. They could see below a large three storey country house and a long winding gravel drive with lights running along the edges.

The shuttle landed almost silently and fully stealthed in the field adjacent to the house. They all climbed down and exited the back ramp.

"I think just John and I should go and see them first" said Paul. "We don't want to overwhelm them completely on the first visit."

"No problem" said Arawn.

"Is that ok Izz?" asked Paul

"No problem" she echoed Arawn making Paul smile. She was picking up more and more human speech and even behaviour.

Paul and John walked down the ramp and into the field, the ramp closed behind them. Paul still had his long coat on and they trudged through the soggy grass and up to the house.

John rang the door bell. A man answered and beckoned them in.

"I believe Mr Summers is expecting you gentlemen" he said. "Please follow me"

Wiping their feet on the huge deep piled foot mat, they followed the 'butler' into a very British lined drawing room. There was the compulsory large fireplace with a log fire burning merrily. A man in a suit and tie, in his early sixties stood up from one of the wingback chairs and walked over holding out his right hand.

He said "Thank you Jenkins that will be all for tonight"

"Very good sir." Jenkins replied and left the room closing the door behind him.

Paul recognised the man's voice as 'Mike' the person they'd spoken to earlier. He shook hands with John then offered to Paul who took his hand and shook.

"Thanks for seeing me at such short notice" he said.

"Well now, anyone that can get from Exeter to here in forty five minutes is probably worth seeing." He laughed.

"Erm I'm sorry , but as this is a matter of national if not international security, can I ask if you have managed to get anyone higher up involved that can listen in? Or better still talk via a video link?"

"Yes he has Mr Arwyn" a voice said from the wall opposite the fire where a screen was winding down and a projector appeared from the ceiling. It was the Prime Minister of the UK Owen Woodford.

"Mr Summers called me and explained what he knew so far. And suggested I might want to listen in? So please, carry on Mr Arwyn. I have twenty minutes."

"Thank you sir." said Paul.

He began with a potted history of the Madden, The Tylvor, and the fact that they had witnessed a Tylvor observation ship leaving as they had arrived.

He explained the Prophecy and the existence of Division 2. He told the PM about the flotilla of Tylvor ships that had appeared in the Coloon system a few days ago. Their encounter with the Altarrians, he told him of the plan the Madden had created and about the hidden fleet and he demonstrated some of the features of his flight suit.

He left out telepathy, Izzy, the medical advances and a few other pieces.

By the time he finished nearly forty minutes had passed.

The PM looked at Paul.

"Well so far I have just your word for this Mr Arwyn. Do you have any actual proof of the danger we are in?"

"I have a video we created prior to this meeting. Max can you download it to the PM's computer?"

"That is completed Captain"

"If you check the desktop of your computer sir there is a video file. Please watch it."

"How did you manage that? I thought these computers were hack proof?" He was a little surprised but he opened the video anyway.

"Sorry Sir, that's madden technology way ahead of ours."

"So if this is all to be believed Mr Arwyn, what do you think I can do? It is a very good video by the way, but I'm sure a good CGI specialist could create the same thing?"

"Rally support amongst our allies' sir? We need to recruit soldiers, crews for the ships etc and take the fight to the Tylvor."

"Well that remains to be seen Mr Arwyn while I do not doubt what you have experienced, and the impressive suit you wear. I'm sorry but at this moment in time I have other more important things to do. Goodnight Mike."

And that was it he was gone leaving Paul speechless.

"How can he not see the danger we're in" he said angrily. "The idiot, bloody politicians" he spat

"Steady on. John here has vouched for you I would say the PM gave you a fair hearing. Now if you want it to go any further then can I suggest you collect some more proof and send it to me, John has my details. In the meantime it's late and I have a very busy day tomorrow."

They walked to the door and out into the rain.

"How can he be so fucking stupid?" Paul yelled at the weather.

"Come on calm down Paul. I know we'll just have to collect some more proof and come back. I'm not defending him here, but as far as the PM's concerned he doesn't see a threat yet."

"That's the problem I don't think we've got the time. The Tylvor could be here with a fleet in less than 9 days. So we've got to try something else."

"Well let's get our skates on then."

"Do you want to come with us?" Paul asked.

"Damn right I do" he laughed. "I wouldn't miss this trip for the world! And it might just come to that" he laughed again.

Paul grinned. "Not if I can help it"

They climbed back into the shuttle and took off vertically. Paul was angry and gave it maximum thrust blowing branches and debris all over the drive of the house.

It took ten minutes to achieve orbit. Johns face when he saw the Maxsar was a picture.

But when he got on board he was stunned. They showed him to his quarters just next door to Arawn's. He and Izzy made friends straight away.

"There is something you might want to know John. I haven't mentioned it yet because it isn't relevant to the defence of Earth."

"Ok…" said John slowly "sounds interesting."

"It is. You remarked how healthy I looked. I am totally cured, there are medical facilities on board that, removed the plates in my leg, repaired my broken vertebrae, stopped my dependency on opiates and I am pain free for the first time in nearly three years. Oh and they can regrow limbs…" he let the last part hang in the air.

John had been listening and shaking his head at what Paul had had done. Then the penny dropped and he stared at Paul.

"You're not winding me up are you? Not about this?"

"No Max told me they can regrow limbs. Using your own DNA they construct a limb in situ. It is scar less, and painless, but apparently there can be itching oh, and it can take you a while to get used to it again. Honestly I'm not pulling your leg?"

They both groaned at that one.

"Have a think about it. I am told the process can take up to four hours depending on the severity."

"Yep thought about… I'm in" he said.

"Ok follow me then" said Paul smiling.

Paul, Max and John walked to the medical bay.

"How do we do this one Max?" Paul asked.

"We need to use the reconstruction pod in bay three" She said walking over to a slightly different looking medical couch.

"Please lay down on this couch, John" she said.

"This is not going to hurt right?" He said laughing nervously.

"No" said Max. "But the skin may be irritated for a while."

"Ok" he said. "trousers off?" he asked as he hopped onto the couch."

"If you wish" She said and stood watching John

"Erm do you mind turning around?" he said sounding embarrassed.

Paul burst out laughing. "Sorry John I forgot to mention Max here is not a flesh and blood lady; she is the ships AI in a mechanical body. She is not the slightest bit interested in checking you out." He laughed again

"What? B-but she's so real." He stuttered clearly surprised.

"It is true; I am not interested in you in any sexual way John"

"Well there's an ego deflator…" He laughed and removed his trousers, his prosthetic leg and got onto the couch.

"Please lay still" she instructed.

The couch completed a total body scan. Max checked the results and pressed a few areas on the screen. The lower half of the couch side grew outwards, upwards and curved over to the other side creating a clear dome over John's lower legs forming a seal across his upper thighs

The dome shimmered and shined as the end of johns stump began to glow. The skin some muscle and nerve tissue were slowly peeled back and dissolved away to reveal the ends of his tibia and fibula. To Pauls surprise and Johns who was managing to watch, there was no blood. The bones began to glow and then grow from their centres. Small amounts at a time; the marrow began to form, a red shiny mass then the hard white bone around it. As the bone and marrow grew down towards the foot, veins, arteries, nerves, lymph nodes, muscle and skin all began to form from the centre of the leg outwards and followed the growth of the bones downwards.

Paul looked at John who had finished marvelling and was looking slightly paler than before. He was now lying down and had closed his eyes.

"Can we make the dome opaque?" Paul asked Max.

"Yes captain" she said and the growing disappeared under a solid white cover.

"Thanks for that" said John. "I wasn't sure how to take it" he chuckled.

"One step at a time?" suggested Paul

John groaned "Always with the crap jokes. They've not changed"

They both laughed.

"Do you need anything?

"Water perhaps?" he asked.

"No worries" said Paul. There was a replicator nearby so he ordered up a glass of cold water and took it to John.

After a while Paul looked at the console "Looks like you'll be cooked in about 25 minutes. Do you want me to hang on?"

"Yes please. So what do you think we should do now?" John asked.

"With regard to the big picture?" replied Paul.

"Yes."

"As I see it," Paul said "it looks like the only way the government will take it seriously is if they are under immediate threat, but by that time it may be too late. The Tylvor military is ruthless and efficient. I am really worried they'll simply turn up and obliterate the planet, then what?"

"Can we defend it using the Maxsar?" asked John.

"If they sent perhaps 3 patrol boats and 2 frigates, that's the most we could handle on our own, but even then it'd be touch and go. If they send more, then were screwed."

"What do you think the time scale is?"

"Max and I are of the opinion that if they turn around the surveillance data quickly and this means getting it to a Tylvor called Daghishat they could be here in as little as nine days"

"Shit" Said John

"Exactly" said Paul.

"I have had a bit of a hail Mary idea." He said.

"It's possible that there is a technologically advanced civilisation on the other side of a passage point through which we sent the Altarrians. It's got to be worth looking? That's it, that's all I can think of. Otherwise we hang around here, launch the 4 fighters and the 2 shuttles we have via remote control and use the Maxsar as best we can to defend earth. I don't hold out much hope that we would survive long."

"It sounds like the only option. How long would it take?" John asked.

"Well, interestingly" said Paul "We could get there in just under two days That leaves us with four days to try and drum up some help and two and a half days to get back, allowing for slower ships."

He paused.

"So all we have to do is find anyone there that could help, and then convince them to fight for a species they don't know, have no links with and have no allegiance to? Easy." Paul laughed ironically.

"The silver lining being, that once they have finished laughing at us, we could be back in time to go down defending the planet"

"How very British" John said. "It gets my vote if I get a vote that is."

"There's something else I need to look at before we get going. Max, is there any way we can patch the vault sensors into the UK early warning system at Fylingdales?"

"Just a moment Captain" she paused then said. "Yes that is possible it will extend the radars current range from 3000 miles into space, as far as the passage point near the Kuiper belt an increase of approximately 4.4 billion kilometres.

"And it'll give them some warning if the Tylvor return."

"Indeed. However, you will need to inform them, they may not take too kindly to our interference."

"Hum, yes you may be right. Can you contact AVM Jameson at UKSC please? Hopefully he'll remember me."

UKSC? AVM?" John asked.

"United Kingdom Space Command and Air Vice Marshall" Paul whispered.

"Connecting now captain" Max replied.

The medical bay speakers played the sound of phone ringing.

"Hello? Who is this and how did you get this number?" said a male voice.

"Is that AVM Jameson, Phil Jameson?" asked Paul

"Yes who is that?"

"It's Wing Co Arwyn, from 617 Squadron? Do you remember me?"

"Paul of course I do, how are you? How are the injuries coming along?"

"They're really well actually. Unfortunately not a social call, do you have five minutes, and is there any chance you could get hold of your leading radar specialist to listen in too?"

"I suppose so, what's it about?"

"It's currently within my power to grant a gift to UKSC Fylingdales. There is no charge and no detriment to your current capabilities in fact you might want to think of it as an enhancement to the current system."

"Well this is all highly irregular but, hold on a minute." He said

Paul was put on hold for about a minute

The AVM came back on. "Right I've got one of our boffins on the line as well his name is David Williams so fire away"

"I have come into the possession of some very advanced technology that can extend the range of the Fylingdales radar." He said

"Extend it by how much?" David asked. Sounds like a bit of a nerd by the eagerness of his question Paul thought.

"Oh, approximately 4.5 Billion Kilometres."

There was an ear splitting hoot of laughter at the other end from David, the AVM didn't say anything.

"Is this a joke?" David asked.

"No" said Paul. "Would you like a demonstration?"

"Yes please this should be good" He said.

"Where are you at the moment?" Paul asked

"I am in the main control room?" David replied.

"Is there a particular desk or console I should direct the information to?" Paul asked

"Yes Lima12?" he said beginning to sound less dismissive.

"Max if you would?"

"Yes Captain, relaying data and overlapping systems now."

There was a pause then a "Fuck me!"

"David, language please. What happening?" interrupted the AVM

"Erm, I think you'd better get down here sir. Can you hold on please Mr Arwyn?" He asked.

"No Problem" Paul smiled.

A few moments later he could here AVM Jameson talking to David at his console. "It's incredible! I am actually looking at the Kuiper Belt, That's bloody Pluto!" he was astounded.

"Hello, Paul?" The AVM came back on the line

"Yes sir?"

"This is incredible, but why would we need this when we are tasked to watch for ICBM launches form Russia?"

"I'm afraid you are going to have to watch for a lot more than that from now on. You are currently synchronised with 7 sensor centres placed around the world. They are Alien technology and their power and sensitivity, well you can see for yourself what that is like. This is a case of not only national security but World security. We are expecting very unfriendly visitors from another part of the galaxy in approximately 9 days time. The world powers need to know of their arrival. Unfortunately there is nothing Earth can do to defend against them. That's what I and my team are trying to change. If you can keep some eyes on that console and alert everyone you need to as and when anything appears that's all I can ask of you."

"Well… I'm stunned. We have seen some strange things here in the past, but what you're saying is not a total surprise and I can spare this console so that isn't a problem. I'm sure the Americans are going to be livid about you being able to hack in to the system apparently at will but that's something I'll handle."

"Thanks Phil. If word of what I have just said gets out to the public then it'll be chaos so from your perspective none of this goes further than you and David and maybe no more than a couple of others for now?"

"I Agree. Obviously I will have to inform Whitehall, but I will make sure it's for certain eyes only." The AVM said.

"Thanks. And good luck."

"Thank you for the data and good luck at your end." Phil said.

The line went dead.

"Well I think that's as much as we can do here." He said

"Max can you get us underway please, maximum Warp?"

"Sorry Captain what is a…Warp?" she asked.

"Doesn't matter" he chuckled "Can we get underway at our fastest acceleration please? Thanks"

John smiled.

"See? All the best phrases are taken!" Paul said. "Shall we go and join the others?"

Back at South Lawns Mikes phone illuminated and vibrated at him. It was the PM again.

"Sir?" answered Mike

"Mike. I'm quite interested in the technology I saw this evening we have been given access to some of it up at Fylingdales I'm told. Can we put someone on it and try and get control of it please? Right away, there's a good chap"

"Yes sir, although I'm not sure where we should look as in, I don't think it's actually on Earth sir?"

"I'm sure you'll sort it Mike, crack on, there's a good fellow" and he rang off.

"What a stupid twat." Mike cursed.

"How does he expect me to do that? Oh well ours is not to reason why etc. etc." and busied himself at his desk doing whatever MI6 people did.

The Tylvor patrol ship had arrived back at the forward operating base for Tylvor ships in this sector. There were at least a dozen ships gathered around the station. Which itself orbited a barren rocky planet called Marth. It wasn't a fun posting for the Tylvor. There were no inhabited planets in the area and even its sun was a cool one an M1V type producing little heat at the distance Marth was located. It was an ancient system; all of the usual interstellar debris had long been hovered up by the gravity of the sun or the only gas giant.

The captain contacted his base commander to deliver the report on Earth but was intercepted by a Div2 representative who demanded he send the report to him immediately. There was no love lost between the regular navy and Div2 so the captain of the patrol ship didn't hurry. An hour later he sent the report.

The Div2 officer forwarded the report to the Tylvor homeworld for the attention of Daghishat himself and waited.

Daghishat was enjoying a relaxing massage from one of his slave girls when his assistant Azrail knocked on the door.

"Come!" he shouted.

"My Lord, the report from Earth as requested."

"Spare me the details, what are the findings?" he mumbled from his face down position on the massage table.

"Erm, essentially nothing has changed since the previous report fifteen years ago. They have no space travel, no unusual technologies etc. etc."

"Hmm" He grunted sitting up and waving away the masseuse. "Why can't the Navy do what their supposed to?" he muttered angrily. He'd now have to go and see or at least speak to chancellor Kedron himself.

"You're dismissed" he said waving Azrail away. The assistant bowed turned and left the room closing the door behind him.

"Computer, get me Chancellor Kedron." He demanded.

"Trying to connect you now sir."

He sat in his robe at his desk, tapping his fingers on the desks surface irritably. The comms call was finally answered.

"Daghishat..." said Chancellor Kedron. "To what do I owe this interruption?"

Daghishat writhed in hatred at the attitude Kedron had towards him. Actually Daghishat hated almost everyone. But Kedron especially, he treated Daghishat with the utmost contempt as if he was something he had trodden in. Daghishat had an important role to protect the empire but no, Kedron didn't see it that way did he. Oh no, Kedron was the Emperors favourite, well, Daghishat was working on that wasn't he yes, he'd show Kedron who he was disrespecting. It may take a while but things were moving.

"Chancellor Kedron." Daghishats voice oozed respect and affability. He was an excellent sycophant when he wanted to be. "I hope you are well?" He asked

"Yes, yes as well as can be expected, now what do you want?"

"A planet has come to my attention from leads I have been following. They are a primitive race, no space travel, no interesting technologies and in fact very little else going for them at all. We have no interests there as far as I am aware."

"Cut to Daghishat I am a busy man" Kedron interrupted.

Daghishat bit his lip and managed to not let his obsequiousness slip.

"But of course Chancellor. I would like to completely eradicate the, I believe they are called Humans?" he paused slightly.

"There is a 17.337% probability they may have something to do with the Prophecy. Might I add, Chancellor, that 17.337% is the highest our analysts have predicted for many years and prudence is probably the wise option here."

He stopped waiting for the chancellor to reply.

"Oh very well, take 6 ships that is all I can spare at the moment and need I remind you that using nuclear weapons is not financially justified? We may need to occupy the planet at some point in the future so do not irradiate it. Kinetic weapons only please."

"Thank y…" but he had closed the line.

"One day…" Daghishat muttered. "Just you wait."

"Computer, get hold of Commander Megaira."

"I am calling now sir."

This time Megaira answered within 3 seconds.

"My Lord?"

"Megaira, have your ships turned around and reroute to Earth here are the coordinates." He typed them into his console and pressed send.

"I want you to bombard all major settlements and any technology sectors you can find. Unfortunately we cannot use nuclear weapons due to the expense so Kinetic weapons only. They should be destructive enough? Shouldn't they?"

"Indeed my Lord. One of our Frigate Kinetic weapons is enough to create the same devastation as a 10 kiloton nuclear device. It may take longer as we may need to reload form time to time."

"How long do you think?"

"It is 4.5 days travel plus sub light each way and I would estimate 7-10 days almost constant bombardment, to be thorough my Lord. I will also need to take a supply vessel to reload with kinetic weapon rounds."

"Yes that should be fine." He enjoyed the thought of the suffering it would bring. A shame he wouldn't be able to see it firsthand. Still he would enjoy the holo reports when the fleet returned.

"See to it Megaira. I would see the reports on your return."

"Yes my Lord" Megaira signed off.

Daghishat sat back and smiled to himself. Another problem dealt with he thought. Now, where is that slave girl? He thought.

Chapter 11

Thirty minutes later John was sitting up with both his legs hanging over the side. He was wiggling his new toes and laughing with tears in his eyes. He rotated the foot round and around.

"Well here goes" he said and inched himself off the couch. His new foot touched the floor. He laughed again.

"What?" asked Paul.

"The floor is cold" he said laughing again. He stood up straight favouring his old leg. He gingerly put more weight onto his new leg.

Then he took a step, stumbled slightly but caught himself. He took another step, then another until he let go of the couch and walked in a circle back to the couch laughing all of the time.

He bounced a little on his new leg. "Oh my god this is incredible. It's as if it had never been missing. I can't thank you enough" he said.

"There is one way you can. You can accept my offer and become Colonel of our Marine contingent?"

"How many marines?" he asked.

"Well, there's you, that's a start." Said Paul and laughed.

John laughed. He offered his hand and said "I would be proud to accept Captain."

"Welcome aboard Colonel Manning" he said.

13 hours later and after an excellent night's sleep they were traversing the Coloon system in stealth while the scan results came in.

"All clear captain." Max reported.

"Thanks Max."

One of the other consoles on the bridge had a new occupant. Colonel John Manning had taken his position to the right of Arawn and below Pauls command chair. It wasn't really confirmed yet what role if any he could take on board, as he was a soldier rather than a sailor or an airman.

A flight suit had been made for him the same as everyone else and he loved its capabilities. He currently sat at the console with his head completely encased in the protective hood that was used for emergency decompressions or when exposed to hostile atmospheres. He was rotating his head around holding his hand up and looking at it he was, presumably getting used to the different vision applications, night vision, infra red etc. Paul chuckled to himself watching John doing deep breathing exercises as if he were wearing diving gear.

John had, for the moment declined the telepathic part of the gene therapy, but had accepted the treatment to "turn on" the technical genes so that he could operate Madden technology.

His name badge said Col. J Manning Marine Cmdr. and he had three bars on his shoulder like Paul. Technically, although they were in different branches of the military, they were both the same rank. But on board ship Paul was the commander. On the ground in a military situation, John would command.

"Let's speed things up Max. Full acceleration please"

"Yes Captain" she replied

The tone of the engines changed and he could feel a rumble throughout the ship. The display showed their destination as a green dot and ETA was 45 minutes.

"John, are there any education course you might like to take? Now would be a good time." Paul asked.

"Yes probably. I wouldn't mind doing some research into Tylvor ground tactics?" he said.

"Max have we got anything on the subject?" Paul asked.

"Yes there are 75 different modules Captain"

Paul was stunned "… 75?" he asked incredulously

"Indeed it was deemed an essential subject for Madden tacticians in order for them to become proficient. However, it did not do us much good in the long run." She said sounding downbeat.

"Well, let's bring a fresh perspective to it shall we?" said John. He stood up and left the bridge.

The travel through the passage point to Thastea was uneventful.

The Thastea system was bigger than any yet. The sun was similar to Sol but a little warmer at G3V there were twelve rocky planets and two gas giants. Two of the planets were in the 'Goldilocks Zone' One of which had a mostly temperate climate the other, which was nearer the sun was hotter bit still habitable in the higher and lower latitudes.

The Thasteans had developed space travel a little sooner than most other civilisations because of the proximity of another planet that was habitable. It had spurred them on and around 200 years earlier they managed to get off their homeworld colonise their second planet and find the Type II passage points. There were two other type II passages heading away from Thastea.

Paul could see on the screen, at least a dozen ships plying their way between the two planets their respective moons and the asteroid belt further out. There were two ships in close proximity to the passage point exit presumably on picket duty.

"Max please make us visible and send a general hail." Asked Paul

"Done" she replied.

Immediately to their right one of the picket ships powered up turned and sped towards the main planet.

"Incoming transmission captain from the second Thastean vessel." Max said.

"Let's hear it".

"...vessel, please heave to and prepare to be boarded. I repeat this is Captain Smaltar of the Thastean ship Grantis.

Unidentified vessel, please heave to and prepare to be boarded."

"They speak English?" He asked.

"Sorry. No I translated for you."

"No don't apologise. Keep if going please and thanks. Can I reply?"

Max paused. "Channel is open go ahead."

"Captain Smaltar, I am Captain Arwyn of the Madden ship Maxsar. We come in peace I wish to speak to your government on an extremely urgent matter concerning the Tylvor. We have nothing to hide. So please send your boarding party. We are heaving to now."

"Max, bring us to a halt and tell them where to dock please."

"Yes sir, Hangar 1 would be best as their docking equipment is not compatible with ours."

"Very good thanks." Paul replied.

"John, will you come with me? Tool up, although let's keep it just to pistols I think."

"Ok I'm right behind you." He replied.

Paul had had a gun locker installed on the bridge to save time in situations like this. They retrieved a pistol each and went to meet their guests.

Hangar 1 was cold. "Max how far away *are* they?" Paul asked impatiently.

"Approximately 10 km Captain they should break the shield in 2 minutes."

"Ok... god I hate waiting like this. Anyway best behaviour we must give a good impression"

"Look at you the diplomat." John sniggered.

"Oh shut up" Paul said smiling a little, he looked to the shield as the Thastean ship broke through.

The vessel was small about the size of a C130 transport. It landed smoothly a ramp at one side extended and the side door opened. Two personnel appeared. They were most unusual looking.

They were green skinned with a large head. The nearest thing Paul could think of when describing their features was a Tapir with a long almost prehensile nose above their mouths. They had large brown eyes and large ears that could swivel, bipedal with legs articulated like birds. The really outstanding feature was their four arms. Two powerful arms extending from the shoulders either side of the neck, similar to humans, ending in three fingers and a thumb with some very menacing looking large, sharp claws attached. They also had two smaller arms and hands extending from the chest. It was most odd watching them walk towards him. They stopped about 3 metres away. He noted that they carried their rifles in their front arms leaving their larger arms free. They wore a flight suit or uniform that covered their bodies completely.

They spoke with a base guttural language. Max provided a translation through the speakers in the neck area of his suit.

"What species are you and what is your business here?"

"We are human" he said indicating himself and John. "We come in peace I wish to speak to your government on an extremely urgent matter concerning the Tylvor." His voice came out of the speakers in his suit in Thastean it was so odd. He tried not to speak too loudly and drown out the translation.

"Your ship will remain here and you will accompany us to our planet." Said the Thastean

"That is not acceptable. I need access to my ship."

"Then return from where you came or be destroyed." He said.

Paul glanced at John who shrugged.

"Max can you meet us in the hangar bay please? John, militarily you're in charge until I return." Paul said.

"Yes Captain" he said

"I am waiting for a member of my crew that will translate for me. Is that allowed?"

The Thastean paused then grunted. Which Paul took as an affirmation?

"Ok..." he thought... good start!

They all shuffled around staring at the floor or the ceiling for a couple of minutes while waiting for Max.

Finally the hangar door opened and Max walked through.

The demeanour of the Thasteans seemed to change slightly. Paul wondered if they could detect she was not made of flesh and blood? Odd he thought.

"Right lead the way please sir!" Paul waved at the Thastean. Who turned and marched onto the ship.

They soon got underway. It took almost an hour to reach their planet but Paul was quietly impressed by the ship. It seemed fast, and sturdily made.

Looking through a window in the side of the ship, Paul could see Thastea below them. It looked quite beautiful, different to Earth, less water and not so many clouds but huge swathes of green. Not too much industrialisation or climate warming, then, he thought.

They landed at a busy spaceport or airfield which seemed to be attached to a smart gleaming high rise city. There were other ships like the one they were on dotted about and some larger ones further away. Ground vehicles ran around, that appeared to be servicing the ships. He could see materials on trailers being moved either by hand or by what he thought looked like large robots.

As they disembarked one of the large robots walked by, it had two legs and two arms to which were attached various tools he then noticed a Thastean sitting in a cockpit in the torso towards the top 'driving' it? What a good idea he thought. We need to get some of them and filed that thought away.

A ground vehicle was waiting. It was like a large Earth van with a sliding side door and windows all round. They got in, there was nowhere to sit, but there were grab rails hanging from the roof he took hold and they moved off smoothly. The journey took about twenty minutes, out of the spaceport and into the main city.

They pulled up at a large domed building. The square outside was busy with Thasteans presumably going about their business. He and Max got out and waited for their escort.

Paul noticed the Thasteans closest stop and stare muttering to each other.

"I suppose they've never seen Aliens before?" laughed Paul

"I think they are staring at me". Paul looked at Max then at the Thasteans.

"Hmm looks like you're right. What's that all about?"

The escort whose body language had changed since Max had appeared. Bowed and pointed and asked that they move towards the building.

They entered the domed building and Paul gasped at how wonderful it was. The dome itself stretched for hundreds of metres in all directions. It was not totally transparent it admitted some outside light, but the patterns and colours of the material created a mesmerising kaleidoscopic effect. He couldn't take his eyes off it. The Thasteans were good architects he thought.

"Captain this way please?" Max was speaking to him. He hadn't heard her as he'd been lost in a reverie staring at the dome.

"Sorry, yes."

"Can you ask them where were going?" Paul said.

A conversation ensued between Max and the Thastean who appeared to be in charge of their escort.

"He says that our arrival is quite a surprise and the Council security committee want to see us as soon as possible." She said.

"Ok, I hope that's a good surprise!" he muttered as they continued walking.

Five minutes later they were sat in a reception room with chairs around the edges and tables in the centre.

An armed Thastean remained on guard at the entrance. Paul caught him looking at Max several times but he looked away when he thought he was being observed.

"They obviously like you" he said smiling.

At that moment another door slid aside and two Thasteans entered. One was wearing what Paul could only describe as lederhosen and huge black boots that clumped as they walked. To Paul he looked ridiculous, he almost laughed out loud but managed to bite his tongue. Oh dear he thought not a good start.

The lederhosen clad Thastean began to speak directly to Max. She appeared a little confused. She replied and the Thastean made a small movement of surprise as if taken aback and looked at Paul.

"I apologise for the mistake Captain Arwyn" the Thastean said."I was not aware the Ancient ones served others?" and he bowed awkwardly.

"Wait, what? Ancient ones? Sorry you have me at a loss. I don't understand." said Paul.

"The Madden are revered in our society. We did not realise there were any left in the Galaxy, my apologies for the lack of respect in welcoming you properly" he said again talking directly to Max. "I am Gathrar, secretary to the Thastean security committee at your service." And he bowed to Max and Paul.

The penny dropped, so he quickly thought to Max

"Play along. They obviously think you, as a Madden, should be in charge. But telling them the truth at this point will not get us anywhere. So if you can think of some reason why I would be in charge over a Madden then let them know"

Max spoke at length to Gathrar. Who nodded, looked at Paul a couple of times then bowed at him and said.

"My apologies again Captain. Please follow me. The committee are anxious to meet you. News of your arrival has spread quickly." He said pointing behind Paul, to a small crowd of onlookers who were gawping slightly at Max.

They walked through the door and into a larger chamber with a semi circular desk area facing them and two tables and chairs in the centre.

Seven Thasteans were already sat on the other side of the semi circle facing them. Like Gathrar they all seemed to be wearing the lederhosen and big clunky boots.

"Oh boy." Paul thought trying not to smile too broadly.

Paul, Max and Gathrar walked to the desks in the middle and stopped.

"Show time" whispered Paul.

Max smiled. She said in a low voice. "The Thasteans are good people one thing you should know, they appreciate honesty above all else."

"Ok I'll keep that in mind"

"Greetings from Earth" Paul opened with.

"My name is Paul Myrddin ap Arwyn. And I come seeking your help."

Once Max's translation finished a murmur ran through the committee. The Thastean sat in the centre spoke.

"Greetings, I am Althar." He said "I am the president of this committee. We are all extremely honoured by your visit. The

Ancient ones have not been seen in over 1500 of our years. Your names they are Ancient names?"

"Does he mean Madden?" Paul thought to Max

"Yes captain"

Paul noticed Althar stiffen slightly as he was thinking to Max.

"Can they hear us?" He thought

"Judging by the presidents' reaction it is a possibility"

Paul thought he'd give it a go so, he thought. Broadcast mode.

"Greetings to you all."

They all stiffened and gasped. Turning to each other they talked quickly and animatedly with much gesticulating of both sets of arms claws flying. Wow, Paul thought I wouldn't want to get too close.

Althar spoke

"You have the gift?" he said.

"Do you mean telepathy?" Paul asked.

"Yes. Certain amongst us can sometimes hear thoughts of our fellow Thasteans. We do not have the ability to project thoughts towards others as you have just done, but occasionally in moments of acute stress thoughts are violently thrown out of our minds and they are heard by others." Said Althar

"All of the members of the security committee have this gift. But to meet another race, other than the Ancients who have the full powers is an honour indeed." He continued "Also your name it is an honoured Ancient name is it not?"

Paul looked at Max. She thought *"They are names of the Madden crew if you remember?"*

"Yes they are Mr President." Paul replied.

"So, how can we, the Thasteans, help the Ancients?"

Paul wondered how to broach the subject that there weren't any Madden left, Max was a robot, and he was human from Earth who needed help.

"Mr President, members of the Security committee, I can only be honest with you. Yes I am named after the Ancients that visited our Planet a long time ago. They left what we call vaults hidden all around our planet with the intention of returning and making contact in order to try and recruit help to fight the scourge that is the Tylvor." He paused.

The committee all nodded at the mention of the Tylvor. One or two made signs with their hands as if to ward off evil spirits Paul smiled.

"Until now, we on Earth have been spared the attentions of the Tylvor. Mostly because we have not achieved the level of technology they deem necessary for close attention. For that I am grateful. However, recently the Maxsar, the ship we arrived in, of which I am proud to be Captain arrived at our planet."

"At first I knew and cared nothing about it, I was in a pit of despair with personal health problems and addiction to pain killing medication slowly dragging me down. Then by accident or a twist of fate, I found a Madden device which removed the pain, guided me to one of the vaults on our planet and I met and connected with Max here."

"We, along with three other members of my crew have come here seeking your assistance. Unfortunately we are just one Madden ship against the might of the Tylvor Empire. But we have a plan. There is hope. We met some Altarrians recently who told me of an ancient prophecy that the Tylvor also believe to be true. It goes something like…"

"Hope will arrive carrying the magician. Four companions two similar one ancient one different and young. The damaged one leads. The fair one counsels. The other and the young one support. They will lead a vast armada. An unstoppable army and peace will reign for ten thousand years."

"It turns out that 'Hope' is what the word Maxsar means in Madden. My name is Paul Myrddin ap Arwyn. Myrddin is the name of a Madden who appeared among our people hundreds if not thousands of years ago. I lead, Max here advises and counsels, and Izzy and Arawn are the support without which we would not be here." He paused for breath.

He was becoming more impassioned by the minute.

"I ask you, no I implore you to help our planet, could you possibly assign ten of your best ships to return with me to fend off the Tylvor and prevent a catastrophic attack on our civilisation. We have a lot to offer the Galaxy."

He stopped and sat down breathing heavily. He'd never spoken like that in public before then again he had never had so much at stake before.

Althar spoke quietly to his colleagues. Then turned and said "Paul Myrddin ap Arwyn, you speak passionately for your planet. " He turned to one of the guards "Please show our other guests in" The guard turned and opened another door, a moment later Martol and his family walked in.

"Captain, you are here. It is a welcome surprise."

"Martol, so glad you made it here safely. I hope you are well. How are you getting on with the locals?" He thought

"All is fine. We have been busy attempting to convince the Thasteans of your cause"

Paul was shocked.*"Thank you I appreciate it."*

Althar spoke. "We were already partially aware of your existence captain as our guest Martol here, has spoken at length of their prophecy. I am sorry but we cannot give you an answer on the loan of our ships."

Paul's shoulders dropped

"It would need ratification by the whole of the ruling council." Paul perked up; thinking there might still be a chance after all. "However, the ruling council are not known for their quick decision making. This could take days before they decide."

"Your honour," interrupted Paul "forgive me for interrupting, but we only have 4 days before we must leave and return home to try and defend our planet with or without your assistance."

"I understand the need for haste." He replied nodding. He paused, thinking, before continuing. "Is there anything you could offer that may persuade the more reluctant members of our ruling council?"

Paul thought about it. Then he had a brainwave it was logical, yes it could work…

"Have you ever heard the legend about the Madden hidden fleet?" he asked

"I am afraid we have not." Said Althar

"About 4000 years ago the Madden were losing the war against the Tylvor. They came up with a brilliant plan. They created a series of autonomous factories in a star system hidden thousands of light years away. Maxsar, my ship knows how to find the location. There are hundreds of ships, equipment, combat armour etc. ready, waiting to be used against the Tylvor. The only thing that prevented it from happening was the untimely disappearance of the Madden themselves and the deaths of certain key individuals Myrddin, my namesake and Arawn included. I can promise, that if we recover the fleet you and your race would be included in the alliance that will share the resources to rid this galaxy of the Tylvor once and for all"

The committee all talked at once. Max couldn't keep up with the translations. So just stopped and smiled at Paul.

Althar held his hands up for quiet. Then spoke again. "One of our members has heard of this legend and did not believe it. However, he is now of a mind having met Martol and now yourselves that something is happening. Please make yourselves comfortable here we may be some time discussing this."

"Can we bring our ship into orbit sir? I would like to remain with my crew at this time. We will also need to leave quickly if the outcome is not a good one for us"

"Indeed we have no objection Captain. If you return to the shuttle that brought you here they will restore you to your ship."

Paul bowed to the committee. "Thank you Mr President, esteemed committee members. We await your decision."

With that they turned and left the committee room picking up the Thastean escort again. The van was still waiting for them outside the Council building. He noticed finally, that the van was floating slightly above the ground. No wheels nice tech he thought. Perhaps there could be a trade agreement between our two planets?

They climbed in held on and the van took off returning them to the shuttle. An hour later they were approaching Hangar 1 on the Maxsar. They arrived safely. Paul thanked the escort who bowed climbed back on board and took off back to Thastea.

"Well that was a stressful day" said Paul to Max as they walked back to the bridge.

"Yes I feel it also" she said "I would like to say, I thought you spoke well and passionately to the Thasteans. If that was not enough then I don't know what would be" She said smiling.

"Oh, if anything will tip the scales in our favour, it'll be the offer of a share of Madden ships and other technology, not my impassioned speechifying." He said.

They entered the bridge to a whirlwind of greeting from Izzy.

"Dad your home!" she yelled to everyone. Bouncing around him yapping happily.

"Yes sorry I had to leave you Izz. I'll try not to again because we're a team all of us."

"Well?" said John looking at Paul

He exhaled heavily. "I just don't know. They're going to put it to the full Ruling Council. Althar doesn't know how long it'll take so we're stuck here for four days before we have to leave anyway."

"He spoke well." Max said looking approvingly at Paul.

"Thanks" he replied.

"Well, I think we should take our minds off it for a couple of hours with dinner, then a movie night?" suggested Arawn

"Ok" chuckled Paul "But don't expect me to be the life and soul" He shrugged.

"No worries" smiled Arawn.

They spent a couple of hours over a pleasant dinner making small talk, trying to avoid the elephant in the room. Afterwards Paul took off with Izzy for a walk in the park rather than hang around for the movie.

He was glad they had the park. It was wonderful. The dome overhead was currently showing an evening blue, red and pink sky with clouds and a slowly setting sun. He still marvelled at it every time he saw it. He could hear the waterfall in the distance and he caught the scent of some evening flower floating around on the air currents.

I'll just have to tough it out and wait.

The sunlight disappeared and gentle evening lights came on around the park. It looked lovely. He and Izzy walked back to their quarters where he showered, and got into bed. He lay there for what seemed like hours until he finally got off to sleep.

The next three days were mentally exhausting. He didn't know what to do. He walked all around the ship and looked into every nook and cranny. He took one of the fighters out for a flight test, then one of the shuttles just to kill time more than anything.

He took some more submersive courses in various subjects selected at random. One was Madden botany but given that the Madden homeworld had been destroyed it was moot.

He even washed the land rover!

The fourth day dawned. They set a cut off time of midday if they didn't hear anything by then they would make their way back to the passage point.

Paul went for a swim with Izzy. They walked in the park; he went for a jog around the decks. He even found the gym and made a half hearted attempt at a work out. In the end he gave up and went back to the bridge.

Time ticked on and mid day came and went. They had heard nothing from the Council. He had heard from Althar that morning that there was one faction that was being very difficult, but then again they always were no matter what the matter in hand.

Paul finally resigned himself to the fact that the Thasteans were not going to reach a conclusion before the deadline or even just after in this case.

"Max. Let's go, standard acceleration please." He said.

"Yes Captain."

The ships engines roared under their feet as they overcome the inertia of the ship and slowly they began moving away.

The passage point was just over an hour and they made their way towards it. A sense of disappointment and frustration tinged with a little trepidation of what ley ahead.

Paul put all of it from his mind and began to formulate a plan for the defence of Earth.

Chapter 12

"Ok here's what we've got" said Arawn. Showing a 3d hologram of the current weapons they had.

Paul had called a meeting to try and brainstorm a defence plan.

Maxsar had 16 missiles per volley with 256 in total each missile could carry up to six separate self powered warheads. She could reload a broadside in 40 seconds.

"We have a Rail gun which has a reload time of 55 seconds but it's easy for them to dodge it at range. Same with the Plasma cannon its good but only really at close quarters."

"What classifies as close quarters?" Paul asked.

"Up to 50Kms for the plasma cannon and 500kms for the rail gun." Arawn replied.

"That's close. I suppose if both sides are out of missiles then yes."

"We have 4 fighters each with 2 type 1 missiles plus they will be unmanned can we use them as kamikaze drones if it came to it? For maximum effect they can be loaded up with Anti matter warheads."

As far as the shuttles were concerned Paul couldn't think how to get the best out of them other than deploy them as point defence platforms against incoming missiles.

"If we keep the shuttles close to Maxsar then can you control and coordinate the point defence Max?"

"Yes coordinating many ships' point defence is part of my core skills"

"Ok anyone have any ideas? Arawn? John?"

He drew empty looks.

"Ok thanks everyone. I might have the germ of an idea. But if anyone comes up with anything let me know as soon as, thanks."

They all returned to the bridge. They were a few minutes from the passage point.

They passed the event horizon and began their day's journey to Coloon. The feeling onboard was sombre, funereal even.

The next 24 hours were the longest of Paul's life. He did not know what to do. Izzy would sit and gaze at him willing him to be happy. She never left his side for more than five minutes.

They passed into the Coloon system this time Paul didn't hang back they ran full active scans as soon as they crossed over, finding nothing unusual they accelerated at 1000 gees towards the next passage point.

It was going to be close he could feel it. He sensed that the Tylvor were on their way.

They entered the final passage point an hour later. This next leg was twelve hours, but there was still nearly another eight hours from the passage point to Earth although it had been reduced slightly due to the direction of Earth's orbit heading towards this passage point.

As the air Vice Marshal had predicted, the Americans had gone ballistic. How had anyone managed to hack in? Let alone patch in some alien tech no one understood that gave them the results they were seeing. Not that they were looking this particular gift horse in the mouth... but still it irked them. As for the Brits, well they just got on with it.

Where were the ground stations? Could they find them? Could they work out how it worked and what was David Williams doing about it?

How come I always get dumped on? He thought.

It was his shift. He had drawn the short straw and was landed with the night shift.

The Air vice Marshall had managed to keep most of them off his back but he now had a US Air Force major shadowing him at work. There were three British personnel and three US personnel on constant 8 hour shifts monitoring the data on the one console in the main control centre at RAF Fylingdales' UK Space Command.

He still couldn't believe they were watching live data coming all the way from the other side of the solar system.

He had a theory of how it was done and he wasn't too wide of the mark. Quantum entanglement, he was sure that's how the sensors worked. But, he had a long way to go before any Nobel prizes were handed out.

He took a bite of the sandwich he'd brought from the cafeteria for his *lunch*, as he thought of it, even if it was 03:00 hours. Harry or Major Harold Jones of the USAF was sat next to him he was quite nice gut, he'd been in the UK for a year and lived locally with his wife and a daughter, a bit of a techy like him; they'd already had some interesting chats on quantum entanglement and faster than light travel he currently had his head buried in a copy of Science magazine.

David looked up as a beep came from the console. He nudged Max "Shit, Harry look!"

He pointed at the screen. 7 blips had appeared on the screen. They had icons next to each one. The chyron at the base of the screen flashed red. It said 3 Tylvor Patrol boats, 3 Tylvor Frigates, 1 Tylvor supply vessel. Each blip was identified individually.

David picked up a phone and pressed an emergency number. It took him straight to the AVM.

It was picked up within three rings. "Yes?"

"We have visitors, sir."

"Oh shit!" was the reply. "I'll be there ASAP."

AVM Jameson hurried into the control room and straight to David's console. By now the members of the other shifts were also there.

"Is NORAD getting this?" Jameson asked.

"Yes sir, they're looking at the same images." said Major Jones.

"Can someone get me the PM please? And I think Major, you know what to do?"

"Yes sir." He replied. He reached into his briefcase and produced a satellite phone. He pressed his thumb to the screen which was scanned, and then he entered a numeric code. The phone illuminated, dialled a preset number and he held it up to his ear.

"David could hear a faint voice and Harry said "Code Alpha Zulu" Then he said "Yes. Delta, two, Alpha, seven, Yankee, Tango" There was a pause.

He put the phone on speaker mode. A voice answered. "This is General William Bates. What's the current status?"

"General its Air Vice Marshall Jameson here. We have visitors and the president needs to be made aware."

"I am on the way to the Oval office as we speak Air Vice Marshall. Is the Prime Minister available?"

"Yes General, I have him now, and we will patch him through to the group momentarily."

"Good, hold one" They could hear voices being raised in the background. People being told in no uncertain terms, to clear out Now.

"Air Vice Marshall?" The Prime Ministers voice was on the line.

"Please hold sir, we are just waiting for the Chairman of the Joint Chiefs and the President sir."

"Thank you." The prime minister said.

"Gentlemen not a good day, Owen, how are you? I wish we were speaking under different circumstances." The voice of the President came over the speakers.

"Yes Charles, not a good day indeed."

"So what do we know gentlemen?"

The AVM looked at David. Who nervously pointed to his chest and mouthed me?
The AVM nodded.

David cleared his throat nervously. "Erm Mr President my name is David Williams I'm the lead boffin sorry, scientist, at UKSC sir. Approximately 13 minutes ago we picked up 7 vessels, Identified as 3 Tylvor patrol boats, 3 frigates and 1 supply vessel entering our solar system. They are accelerating towards us at a rate that will bring them to Earth in under 4.5 hours."

"We have reason to believe they are hostile. The little information we know at the moment came from ex Wing Commander now Captain Paul Arwyn he is the captain of the alien vessel we know as Maxsar, belonging to a race of people called the Madden. He sent us a report 8 days ago before departing to attempt to recruit another race's assistance in fighting off the Tylvor. As of now we haven't heard anything back from Captain Arwyn Sir."

"Thank you Mr Williams, I am aware of the back story and I have read Captain Arwyn's reports, so gentlemen suggestions?" said President Lambert.

The silence was frightening.

"Anyone?"

"General Bates. Have we managed to create any contingency plans?"

"Sorry sir, we simply didn't have the time, we had a few ideas on paper, such as modifying ICBM's to be able to be launched into space but it has not progressed any further."

"It's Air vice Marshall Jameson here sir, I am afraid our only egg in this rather empty basket is Captain Arwyn. He said his mission was a Hail Mary, and we have not heard anything back yet."

"Shit. Dammit has anyone got anything?" President Lambert exclaimed.

"We could try contacting them and asking to parley?" suggested Prime Minister Woodford.

"Unlikely to get us anywhere Owen, considering the comments about the Tylvor in the reports I read."

"I think we should inform other world governments Charles. I'd want to know, even if it was just to get to say good bye to loved ones."

"That's depressing Owen." replied the President. "But I think you're correct. I will talk to the Russian and the Chinese, can you inform our European Allies?"

"Of course, I'll get on it as soon as we finish here." The PM said.

"I suppose there's not a lot we can do then other than pray Captain Arwyn is successful and returns with help"

"I agree Mr President. A dark day for all of us." said Prime Minister Woodford.

"I will wish you all the very best of luck. Let's hope Captain Arwyn comes through. I must call my counterparts now, I will remain here in the oval office. We'll monitor the imagery from here. Prime Minister, gentlemen, God protect us All."

"Mr President, good luck to all of us." The Prime Minister signed off.

The AVM disconnected the phone as did Major Jones. They all stood around not saying anything. A gloom had descended.

"Well I'm staying here." David said. "I don't actually have anyone to go home to but I know all of you guys do. I think I know where I would rather be if I had the choice."

"Indeed, David, thank you. I think you all need to go home." said Air vice Marshall Jameson.

"There really is no need to stay here and there is nothing any of us can do. David here will monitor the data and lets us know if anything changes. Go, be with your families. That's an order." He smiled a sad smile and waited for the airmen and civilians to leave.

"Keep me up to date if anything happens David." He said as he left the room.

David was alone. He slumped in his chair a sense of dread hanging over him. Had it really come to this was it finally the end of the world?

His whole career had been spent designing, modifying and maintaining the radar system that monitored for ICBM launches from western Russia, for nuclear Armageddon. He had always hoped, and believed that a nuclear war would be averted and it was in the hands of everyone on Earth to prevent it.

But this, this was far worse. The timer on the screen seemed like the remorseless tick of approaching death. Shit, so many things he hadn't done…

Sleeping, swimming and eating. Not the best way to while away the hours but eventually they neared the final exit back into the Sol system.

"Max can we exit in stealth please and passive sensors only."

"Yes captain"

The countdown reduced to zero and they were through, back into Earths system.

It took several painstaking minutes for the sensors to update. The alarms blared.

This time it wasn't a surprise for Paul as much as a stab in the guts. He could see 8 blips on screen. There were 7 labelled as Tylvor, 3 fast patrol boats and 3 frigates, there was also another large vessel labelled as a supply vessel. That puzzled him why would they need a supply vessel?

It suggested they were going to be here for a while? Was that normal behaviour?

"Max can we get a reading from that supply vessel. What is it carrying?" Paul asked.

"At this stage no captain. We will know more in a few more minutes."

"Very well let's keep on doing what we're doing then!" he said it out of frustration.

"Time to Earth for us and the Tylvor please Max?"

"We should arrive in seven hours twenty five minutes 4 hours and fifteen minutes after the Tylvor, Captain."

"Damn! When will they be in range of our missiles?"

"At maximum deceleration we should be able to launch our first salvos 20 minutes before we reach earth."

"OK. Here's what I want to try…"

And Paul explained the plan.

Chapter 13

The Maxsar remained at stealth acceleration. They couldn't afford to alert the Tylvor to their presence.

The Tylvor had moved into position and had surrounded the Earth placing their three frigates over Europe, Asia and North America. But nothing had happened for over three hours. One fast patrol boat accompanied each frigate and the supply vessel was located in orbit above the magnetic North pole.

"Any further with finding out what's happening Max?"

"I can detect routine transmissions between the frigates and the patrol boats but nothing else, apart from the attempt by NORAD to communicate with the Tylvor three hours ago. Also I have managed to work out why they have a supply vessel. The Frigates have kinetic weapons, however they only carry three rounds each so the supply ship is there to replenish."

"So it's likely to be a drawn out affair?"

"What the hell are they waiting for?" Paul paced up and down.

It's a good thing at least they're not firing he thought. But not knowing was driving him crazy.

Commander Megaira was proud of his Flagship, or at least that's how his inflated ego referred to it, and it was what he insisted his subordinate captains called it, much to their own private amusement. He sat in his command chair where he watched the display and read the reports provided by his scanning officer. He had eaten a particularly pleasant lunch and was preparing himself for an afternoon of killing.

He was waiting for as much information as possible, to select the juiciest targets before he opened fire. He figured taking a little time to plan the devastation would be the right thing to do. He saw several large cities and instructed the other two frigates to aim at those. He would coordinate the attack. He liked this kind of battle the best, nothing to do but sit back and enjoy the carnage.

He checked the position of the supply vessel. They would need replenishing after 3 rounds each. That would take at least two hours. He had instructed them to travel directly to the supply vessel immediately after firing their third kinetic round. That should do it he thought.

He glanced at the ships chronometer. They had been in system nearly 8 hours so plenty of time yet. He had told Daghishat to allow for 7-10 days for the operation to be completed. This would be a leisurely job to be enjoyed by all.

"Are you ready lieutenant?" He asked his subordinate.

"Yes sir" snapped his deputy.

"Then send the signal."

A countdown appeared on the bridge main screen it reached zero.

All three frigates let loose their kinetic weapons towards Earth.

Shanghai, St Petersburg and Chicago all were hit. No warnings, nothing, just the instantaneous equivalent of a 10 Kiloton nuclear weapon. Each hit destroyed a five kilometre radius of the centre of each city, and created a blast wave that destroyed or damaged most building up to another 4 kilometres beyond that.

Three cities destroyed in the blink of an eye.

An alarmed Max said "They have launched kinetic weapons sir."

"Damn them all to hell" Yelled Paul.

"Where have they hit?"

"Shanghai, St Petersburg and Chicago." She replied indicating the targeted areas on a map of the earth on the main screen.

"What's their reload time again?" Paul asked.

"65 seconds and they carry three rounds each" said Arawn.

The display showed seven minutes until the launch window of the first Type 2 missiles. They would be able to hit another three cities before the Maxsar was within range of launching anything and Paul wanted the first missiles to be launched stealthily.

"Ok Max lets grab their attention, launch all four fighters and the shuttles please. Let's try and distract them. A slight change of plan, let's keep the Maxsar stealthed.

"Yes Captain"

Paul saw on screen the fighters and the shuttles emerge from the hangars.

He moved Maxsar away to the left and above leaving the six vessels alone for now.

Commander Megaira was relaxing in his command chair enjoying the ruin and devastation when an alarm registered on the main screen.

He couldn't believe his eyes. Madden ships, in this system? No, no, no. That's not right he thought.

"Sensors!" he shouted "Re-scan these new sightings. There must be some error."

"Scanning now sir." came the reply.

"Scans are correct sir there are four Madden fighters and two shuttles on course to intercept us in thirty minutes."

"Divert the other two ships and 2 Patrol boats, intercept and destroy them all."

"Yes sir."

"Continue with the bombardment." He motioned to the weapons officer.

Thirty seconds later. "They have seen our ships captain and are moving to intercept." Max said.

He could see on the screen that two of the Frigates and two of the patrol boats were moving away and heading towards the six madden ships.

Given the capability of the ships shields he didn't think they would last long. However he still had time to put most of his plan into action.

"Launch the three waves of mark 2's please Arawn" He said calmly.

"First round away." He said "Reloading."

He glanced at the reload countdown less than 45 seconds but by god it seemed interminably slow. He refocused on the overall battle. The four Tylvor ships would be within range of missiles in 15 minutes.

"The third frigate has targeted and fired on Berlin captain"

"Bastards!" His clenched fist and pummelled the arm of his chair.

Round two away" said Arawn.

"How many is that?" Paul asked

"32" said Arawn

"OK let's stick to the plan"

"Captain the third frigate and patrol boat are moving away to join the others."

"Ok, finally a stroke of luck at least we'll be able to target all of them without them escaping." He said optimistically.

He knew that the Tylvor still had the edge numerically. The first two frigates and patrol boats were now slowing to allow the other two to catch up. The chances for survival against this number of Tylvor ships were about 50% and unfortunately, The Tylvor commander appeared to know what he was doing.

"Third round away" said Arawn

"Ok launch the missiles from all four fighters together as soon as they are in range."

"Yes Sir." said Arawn.

They waited.

"Launching now" said Arawn

Four new green icons appeared on the screen and moved quickly away from the fighters' icons. A reload timer appeared next to each fighter.

"Launch the second missile as soon as they're ready" Paul said.

He watched the timer countdown to zero

"Second missile away from each fighter" Arawn reported.

A second set of icons representing the second round of missiles sped away towards the Tylvor.

"What a pitiful display." laughed Commander Megaira.

"Destroy those missiles" he said to his weapons officer.

"Yes sir" the weapons officer grinned.

He waited until the first four were within range of the point defence network before opening fire. As soon as the first lasers and kinetic weapons began firing at the missiles they began to fly an evasion pattern. They were getting nearer and nearer to the Tylvor frigate at the front of the formation.

Commander Megaira began to get a little concerned that they hadn't destroyed any yet.

"What is happening, why haven't these pathetic weapons been destroyed yet!" He raged banging his fists on the console.

Suddenly one blew up followed by another a small cheer went up from the Tylvor officers.

"Be quiet you imbeciles" Megaira shouted at his crew.

The point defences continued pouring out hundreds of projectiles and laser bolts. Still the two remaining missiles came on. Until finally only five kilometres away from the first Frigate they were both destroyed.

The commander emitted a huge sigh of relief. "Now fire our missiles" he yelled.

Eighteen missiles streaked away from the Tylvor flotilla heading for the small group of Madden ships. As they came into range the Madden point defences opened up. Straight away they knocked out two missiles but the rest began altering their headings in random directions making things much more difficult.

Max was coordinating the point defences. Paul suggested she concentrate on protecting the fighters as they had the ability to strike back at the Tylvor whereas the Shuttles were not so well armed.

Max had detected a pattern to the movements of the Tylvor missiles and had correctly anticipated such that four more Tylvor missiles disappeared in flashes of light.

Only twelve left Paul thought.

Meanwhile the second wave of four Madden missiles was now approaching the Tylvor. They managed to destroy three but the last one dodged and weaved about until it came within 4.5km of the first Frigate and detonated its Anti matter warhead.

The flash was tremendous sensors went offline for a couple of seconds. When they returned the Frigate was no longer under power and trailed debris and what appeared to be gas was venting from several places along the hull. It fell behind the other Tylvor ships.

"YES!" shouted Paul, Arawn and John all at once punching the air and high fiving. Their celebrations were short lived.

"Captain I am sorry to report but the damaged frigate appears to be reigniting its engines."

Sure enough the damaged vessel, although trailing behind the others, had managed to correct its heading and appeared to be under control and still in the fight.

"Damn... can't we get a break?"

The two flotillas were decelerating. Paul realised that it was crunch time. The remaining twelve Tylvor missiles had been reduced to eight.

"Max, engage the evasive manoeuvres for the fighters and shuttles please."

The six vessels moved apart, unfortunately, each ship would now have to manage their point defence individually. Four of the Tylvor missiles turned and headed for one of the fighters. He watched as the inevitable happened.

Nothing remained of the fighter. Paul wondered absently if it had been the one he'd flown. The other three flung themselves around trying to avoid the missiles. They were fairly successful as the missiles were intended to attack bigger, slower moving targets than fighters. But one more succumbed leaving two fighters and two shuttles.

"I am detecting some unusual energy readings in this sector sir" The sensor officer indicated to his Commander. "It could be a hidden ship sir"

"Alter our heading towards it" Commander Megaira ordered.

"Yes sir, altering our heading."

"Captain they are changing direction away from the fighters and are heading towards us. I think they may have detected us"

"Shit. How?"

"I'm afraid I don't know."

Could anything else go wrong he thought.

The display currently showed the previous launches of stealthed Type II's were almost in position but the sudden change of direction of the Tylvor flotilla would take them away from the area Paul wanted them in. He had to get them back in position.

"Max let them see us and move back on to this heading." He entered the coordinates "We need to get them back on course for our surprise to work."

"Yes sir" she said.

"Commander" The sensor officer yelled. "It's a Madden cruiser sir!" he said as the Maxsar de stealthed.

"Damn it where did they come from. Are there any more?"

"Doubtful sir" said the sensor officer. "We see four Madden fighters and two shuttles. That is a standard cruiser compliment"

"Concentrate all fire on the cruiser. Main laser, kinetics, missiles even our point defence. Notify all of the other ships."

"Yes sir. Although we are well out of range for the laser and kinetics we only have one left sir. The other ships have two each."

"I know full well you dolt. We can still get lucky" he yelled at his weapons officer.

The Tylvorian ships changed their heading to concentrate on the cruiser.

The current range to the lead frigate showed as 7500Km. It seemed so close on the screen yet in reality if Paul was stood on the deck of the Maxsar he wouldn't be able to see a thing.

Oddly he felt it wasn't any different to fighting in the F35 just the scale and time.

"How many Mark II's are left?" Paul asked.

"We have two hundred and eight, with forty eight in flight, stealthed."

"How long will it take to swap out to Mark I's fission?"

"Ninety five seconds"

"Do it. Let's launch a full spread of Mark I's next, fission warheads unstealthed please. Target the Frigates"

The time ticked by slowly. Finally all greens appeared on the display and the tubes launched the Mark I's.

A full spread of 16 missiles leapt away.

"Missiles detected Commander" The sensor officer informed Megaira.

They were now 5500km apart. Sixteen missiles were in bound. "Synchronise point defences shouted Megaira

"Yes sir." The outpouring from all 6 ships of point defence lasers and projectiles was massive. However, the Type I missiles were agile and capable. Nine were hit almost immediately the other seven closed in but only one successfully got close enough to detonate. It managed to cause damage to one of the patrol boats reducing their point defences slightly.

Paul felt the ship shudder and the readout on the display showed the shields had dropped to 92%.

"Max, what do you think that was?"

"I suspect a kinetic round sir"

"Let's try and keep out of their way then? Evasion pattern Delta please." The evasion pattern would cause the Maxsar to move in random directions while at the same time trying to maintain the general direction onwards towards the targets.

"Yes sir" Max said

The Tylvor flotilla was currently at 4000km and closing on Pauls plan fast. They were in a triangular formation the three frigates together forming an arrow head while the patrol boats covered them above and below.

The countdown had begun. All of the 48 stealthed missiles they had launched were currently holding position in a flat circle facing the approaching flotilla. They were positioned so the blast from each warhead overlapped its neighbours the blast diameter would approach one hundred kilometres. Each missile contained six warheads giving a total of 288 antimatter devices.

The Tylvor needed to just come on a little further. Just a bit more said Paul watching the screen closely.

"Sir I am picking up some odd readings between us and the Madden ship?" reported the sensor officer.

"What kind of readings?" He asked

"They appear to be multiple dark energy readings scattered across 100km sir"

"How far ahead?"

"25 seconds sir"

He thought for a second then it dawned on him

"BREAK, BREAK. All ships veer off it's a trap." he shouted

His ship pulled up and curved away from the area in question.

"They've found the trap sir!" Arawn yelled.

"Dammit. Detonate the missiles NOW Max" he yelled.

Multiple explosions detonated almost as one across a vast expanse of space causing the Maxsar's display to dim automatically.

After twenty seconds the display cleared but disappointingly all they had to show for it was one Patrol boat had been completely vaporised and another was now coasting without engines venting atmosphere.

"Bollocks!" shouted Paul. "Shit, shit, shit"

The trap he had hoped would catch at least one or two of the frigates had failed. But better two of the six than none, and one of the frigates had already been damaged.

"Max how did they know they were there?"

"They must have improved their sensors since I last updated my records captain. I am sorry."

"It's not your fault Max. We will adapt."

Using the confusion caused by the trap, the Maxsar's contingent of fighters and shuttles had altered their course and were converging on the Maxsar to help provide point defence.

The Tylvor were by no means finished they had regrouped and were now heading back into the fight.

They outnumbered the Maxsar in kinetic weapons 3:1 and they still had a missile volley of 12 although according to Max's records they only held twelve missiles in total and they had fired 8 so only one more spread to avoid.

"Launch a full spread of missiles Arawn"

The display showed 16 missiles on their way.

Maxsar shuddered twice. This time an amber warning came up on the display. The shields were down to 70%

"Kinetic strikes?" Paul asked.

"Yes captain. They have two kinetic rounds left. This is the biggest problem we face. The Tylvor will try and predict the ships movements and aim accordingly. As we get closer they will be more accurate."

Paul understood. He didn't really want to go toe to toe with the Tylvor as they were outnumbered and eventually the Tylvor would wear them down.

The ship shuddered again only this time it felt different. The shields had dropped to 50%

Paul looked at Max. "Main Laser strike sir they have 3 main lasers as well as the kinetics." She said.

Paul was getting worried now. They needed some luck.

"Are you waiting for anything in particular to use the rail gun Arawn?" he asked unfairly.

"No. It's just that it's easy for them to dodge" he said.

Paul said, thinking out loud. "What if they can't see it coming?"

"Huh?" asked Arawn

Looking at the display the next spread of Madden missiles was approaching the Tylvor point defence.

"Max on my word detonate the missiles. Arawn target one of the frigates with the rail gun and when we blow the missiles fire."

"Ah, I get you" he nodded approvingly "Let's give it a go."

The missiles were 50 Km out when Max triggered them. Again a screen white out.

There was a noticeable boom from the Maxsar and a nudge of gravity as the rail gun fired.

The 15 ton, heavy metal, shaped projectile left the ship at an appreciable percentage of c it passed almost instantaneously through the nuclear blast ahead of it untouched and slammed straight through one of the frigates from stem to stern.

The frigate peeled apart like a banana, debris flying in all directions, small explosions triggered along its length and finally when one of the reactors lost containment, most of the wreckage disappeared in a brief fireball.

There was cheering on the bridge of the Maxsar.

"All right let's not lose focus guys." said Paul.

Commander Megaira was furious he was shouting and raving about 'no good officers' they sent him the dregs. He will execute everyone concerned.

After a minute he calmed down. He focused on the main display. The Madden ship was slowing down. They needed to concentrate on kinetics and laser. The remaining two frigates still had the upper hand here.

"Synchronise our last kinetic and lasers with the other frigate" he bellowed. "I want laser following up the kinetic strike both ships are to concentrate on the same area around the engines.

The remaining patrol boat is to provide close point defence cover."

"Yes sir" the comms officer relayed the information.

The Tylvor concentrated their efforts and fired all four of their remaining main lasers on one area at the rear of the Maxsar. The shields burned a deep dark blue changing to black. Maxsar moved and the targeting was lost but the damage was bad.

Maxsar shuddered they were jostled violently in their seats. The automatic straps had activated and secured them all preventing anyone from being injured even Izzy was now sitting on her podium with her head sticking out of the webbing that had automatically activated.

Alarms blared across the bridge. The previously dead console now illuminated with multiple red flashing icons.

"What's that Max?" Paul shouted above the dim

"It is the Damage control console. It would appear we have suffered a breach of our main armour where the shields failed." She yelled back.

"How bad is it?"

"We have exposure to space on three decks. We have lost two communications arrays, a whole set of sensors and 13 of our missile tubes are now inoperable. Shields are now down to 15% in the targeted area."

"Shit how many more hits like that can we take?" he hollered.

"Preferably none sir." She shouted back.

"Can we kill the alarms please?"

Silence returned to the bridge.

The Tylvor were now within 400 kilometres.

Paul guessed this was now going to become a dog fight. Well he was trained for that.
He wasn't going to go down without at least trying to get one or more of the enemy.

He thought *"flight controls right rail gun control on trigger, throttle left"*

The control stick appeared out of the seats' right hand armrest this time with a trigger control attached at the top and the throttle out of the left arm.

Paul accelerated towards the nearest Frigate, which dodged out of the way and came around up and over the top. He was prepared for it though and using the thrusters he vectored in flight moving the ship in an unexpected direction so that the Frigate lost him.

Paul couldn't see where the other frigate or patrol boat was, when suddenly the whole ship shuddered massively. More red icons on the damage control console. This time sparks and smoke flew from a conduit overhead.

Max reported "Engines one and three are out of action, our last missile tubes are off line. We have Plasma cannon and rail gun anti missile missiles and one point defence turret left captain"

He pushed the throttle forwards to its limit but there was almost no response from the engines. He used the thrusters to move the ship to one side just as a main laser bolt flew past the port side more laser bolts flew past then struck amidships causing even more alarms to trigger.

They were in trouble.

Commander Megaira laughed and clapped his hands. "Well done everyone they are virtually dead in the water."

"Avoid their kinetic weapon. It appears to be still active and disable the plasma cannon. I am going to enjoy…"

He never finished his sentence because his ship was vaporised.

"What the fuck…" said Paul, as he watched a Tylvor frigate vanish in a ball of fire.

An instant later the last surviving Frigate and patrol boats both blew up.

"Max?"

"I don't know sir"

Thirty seconds later after the blast cleared, four ships materialized in front of the Maxsar.

It was the Thasteans.

"There is an incoming communication captain" said Max

"Put it on screen Max" he said.

Security Committee President Althar appeared. "Greetings Captain Arwyn I hope we have arrived in time"

"President Althar. I don't know what to say. You're timing was perfect but, how?"

"A story I will keep for when we meet. I see there is another ship attempting to escape. Two of our frigates are in pursuit they will not get away. Do you need assistance?"

"Max?" Paul asked.

"Thank you for the offer president Althar but the maintenance robots are attending to the repairs as we speak. They should have the engines up and running within 4 hours."

"Please let us know if we can help." said Althar.

"We will. Thank you again." said Paul. "Are you intending to remain here for a while sir?" Pal asked. "I think the civilians on our planet will be in great need of medical and other kinds of assistance. If you are able to"

"We would be happy to oblige Captain. If you can liaise with your planet authorities I can send four of my ships to assist immediately. We shall remain here until you can get underway."

"Thank you. Arwyn out" Paul said and closed the connection.

The straps had released everyone from their seats; they stood up, looking shell shocked but grinning from ear to ear. All five of them came together as one, shook hands and clapped each other on the back; Izzy was yapping and springing around. Paul cuddled her and ruffled her fur. Max joined in grinning broadly.

"That was close" said Paul.

"No shit!" said John and they all laughed again.

Paul contacted the PM and the US president. All four damaged cities were in need of help. They had watched the whole thing unfold via the sensor network.

Paul explained that the Thasteans were unusual looking aliens so not to be too surprised by their appearance. They were good people he added.

Two of the Thastean ships left for Earth where they were joined by the two that had destroyed the supply ship.

The repairs took an hour longer than expected. But they got underway with the Thasteans following at a respectful distance.

Paul explained to them to the PM and the president that they still had a big problem. The Tylvor weren't gone. This flotilla was just a drop in the ocean. They would have to try and figure out a way to prevent the Tylvor from attacking again.

Paul, John, Arawn and Max were sat in the cafeteria eating lunch three days later.

"We have managed to recover a lot of data from the patrol boat we damaged captain" said Max.

"And what has that told us?" He asked

"I have updated my knowledge of Tylvor technology and the current state and extent of the empire and their fleets. I am still processing a lot of information."

"Is there any way we can use this to keep the Tylvor from Earth. Because I have a nasty feeling if we can't keep them away from here they will be back in the next couple of weeks but this time with a much bigger stick!" Paul said.

"Your idea with the type II missiles along with John's suggestion of mines got me thinking. I may have a plan that can prevent the re-materialisation of vessels as they come through the passage point."

"Is this a permanent solution?" he asked."

"I think so yes" she said.

"What's stopping us?"

"Nothing really I thought perhaps you wanted to be here for a while longer?" She replied.

"I will be able to relax better, after I know we can secure the solar system from further attacks at least to give us some breathing room."

"This should work. It will be implemented across the Type 1 passage points only."

"Yes of course. We will be able to use the type 2 passage points." Said Paul

Chicago, Shanghai, St Petersburg and Berlin were virtually gone or at least a ten mile radius of where the kinetic rods had hit were wastelands. A massive crater had appeared at each impact sight. The only silver lining was that there was no radiation or fallout. Although massive plumes of dust had been thrown up into the atmosphere and would cause significant changes to weather patterns for months.

The death toll was over twelve million people in total.

Paul's anger was boiling over as he watched from space. The Thasteans offered medical technology that helped in a huge way. Max was able to replicate vast amounts of drugs of various kinds. Even the pico nanites came in handy to repair damaged limbs. Tens of thousands of people were saved.

The UN seemed to have grown a pair and had coordinated and directed the help of Maxsar and the Thasteans to where it was most needed. The world came together as never before.

Another silver lining, no one seemed to be keen on trying to cover anything up, the story of the Madden, the Tylvor and the Thasteans. The parts played by Paul, John, Arawn, Max and Izzy along with the Altarrians prophecy was all made public, this particular genie was definitely out of the bottle. Almost everyone in the world simply accepted it. In fact the crew of the Maxsar became heroes much to Paul's embarrassment. They were careful not to let anything slip in regard to the hidden fleet. They needed to keep this under wraps for as long as possible.

The only country complaining was Russia. They said none of this would have happened had we not stuck our heads above the parapet. It was all the fault of the West and this was a massive ploy to attack Russia. Most of the Russian people simply ignored what their government said embarrassed by the control freaks in charge.

The Maxsar and two of the Thastean vessels made their way to the passage point from which the Tylvor had emerged.

Max had designed and built two dark energy power sources within four days. They were clumsy looking devices about half the size of one of the shuttles.

Essentially, she had modified a neutron emitter, the same device used to open the passage points. It would disrupt the passage point whenever anything tried to re-materialize at the exit the effect would be instant oblivion. The power source was more or less infinite so the 'batteries' wouldn't need changing as Arawn suggested which got a laugh.

Nice, thought Paul. I'm glad she's on our side.

They hurried to the other passage point and set up the same system there.

Providing the Tylvor didn't discover the type II passage points they should be fine for a while, hopefully. It would give them time to get organised, formulate a plan to find the hidden fleet, get it up and running and finally pay it back to the Tylvor.

Epilogue

Paul was walking through the park with Izzy, they had just completed a swim and Izzy had pestered him until they played a game of ball.

His phone rang.

It was Louise.

He pressed the answer button with a trembling finger.

"Hi" he said shaking slightly.

"Hi." The so familiar voice replied.

He nervously cleared his throat. "So how's things?" he asked.

"I'm ok." She said "How are you? I have seen you on Telly many times these last few days, quite the hero." She said

"Oh not really, just doing what anyone else would have done."

"Yeah right," She said he could hear the smile in her voice. "How are you Paul?" the smile turned to concern.

"If you mean physically and mentally, I'm pretty good… my injuries are completely healed, thanks to amazing Madden medical technology. The addiction to painkillers has also been fixed. Oh and I can talk to Izzy telepathically."

"You can't tell anyone ok?" he hurriedly added.

There was a gasp at the other end and a chuckle. "Seriously?"

"Yes. I can talk to other telepaths. Max, Arawn and Izzy along with one or two of the Thasteans can all hear me. Those that have the full ability can talk back to me as well. It's amazing."

"I'll bet it is" she said

"I'm so glad you are ok." She said.

"Me too"

"That you're ok I mean." He corrected

She laughed "I know what you mean"

It sounded so good to hear her voice and her laugh again. He hadn't realised how much he missed her. Old feelings resurfaced like a tidal wave, overwhelming him emotionally. But it was a nice feeling.

"So what next?" she asked.

He paused for a moment to collect himself.

His voice cracking slightly "I have to go away on a mission to find something. I don't know how long we will be."

He took a deep breath, crossed everything and asked.

"When I return if it's ok with you... could we perhaps... if you want to... you don't have to if you don't want to..."

"Oh for god's sake" she said, he could almost hear her rolling her eyes "Yes, I would love to see you again!" she burst out laughing so did Paul.

End of Book 1.

Dear reader, the series will continue if you want it to, in Book 2 "The Hidden Fleet." So let me know if you enjoyed it or hated it lol. Any comments will be received...

Regards Glyn.

Printed in Great Britain
by Amazon